THE BRYDONS IN SUMMER

The Brydons are a family of enterprising
children, looked after by absent minded
'Marsdie'. There are now 19 stories about
their escapades, which began as radio plays
for B.B.C. 'Children's Hour'.

The children at St Jonathan's Hospital are
taken on an outing to the seaside, which
nearly ends in disaster when Dan, Sam,
Charlie and Juan wander off to look for
treasure on a little island. But on this
occasion Marsdie's forgetfulness proves a
blessing in disguise, and all ends happily.

Also available in Knight Books is *More
adventures of the Brydons*.

D1142668

The Brydons live at One Elm Cottage, Milchester, a village in the north of England. Next door to them at Beechacres is St Jonathan's Convalescent Hospital for Crippled Children, where their mother, Dr Brydon, is the doctor-in-charge.

The Brydons, Roger, Ruth, Simon and Susan who are twins, and Dan, are all looked after by Miss Marsden. 'Marsdie' is an old friend of their mother's. Or perhaps it is more correct to say that the Brydons look after Marsdie, as she is terribly forgetful. Anyway, the arrangement works very well and, as Ruth says, they 'get the best of both worlds' with St Jonathan's next door and their own pleasant home in the adjoining cottage.

We mustn't forget Sam Mitton too, who is Dan's special friend and shares all the Brydon adventures. Indeed, Sam's purpose in life seems to be to get Dan out of their numerous scrapes.

Enjoy yourselves with the gay Brydon family!

Kathleen Fidler

The BRYDONS
in summer

KNIGHT BOOKS
the paperback division of Brockhampton Press

To the memory of Sybil Arundale, whose happy voice in 'Children's Hour'
made 'Marsdie' come alive

ISBN 0 340 04208 7

This revised edition first published 1971 by Knight Books,
the paperback division of Brockhampton Press Ltd, Leicester

Printed and bound in Great Britain by Cox and Wyman Ltd,
London, Reading and Fakenham

First published 1949 by Lutterworth Press
Text copyright © 1971 Kathleen Fidler

Contents

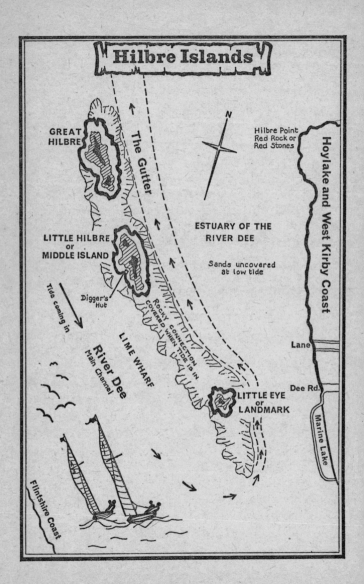

CHAPTER ONE

Ruth throws out a challenge

IT was five minutes to eight on a bright morning towards the end of July. At One Elm Cottage, Milchester, the Brydon family and Miss Marsden were seated at breakfast in the roomy old kitchen with its cheerful brasses and bright red-tiled floor. They were listening with eager interest to the precise voice of the B.B.C. News Reader detailing the weather forecast. His voice ran on: 'Occasional slight showers in the North-West early in the day. Further outlook for Saturday – continuing warm and fine.'

Susan gave a little cheer. 'Hurrah! It's going to be a lovely day for St Jonathan's Garden Party tomorrow.'

The rest of the family nodded happily at each other and Miss Marsden gave a long-drawn sigh of relief. So much depended on the weather being fine. Ever since the holidays had begun, she and the Brydons had been arranging and preparing for a summer fête at St Jonathan's Children's Convalescent Hospital next door at Beechacres, where Dr Brydon, the mother of the Brydon family, was the resident doctor. All the kindly folk of Milchester had been invited and many tickets had been sold, for by this Garden Party the Brydons hoped to raise a sufficient sum of money to take all the little patients of St Jonathan's for a summer outing by motor coach. The many friends of the

Children's Hospital had rallied round them: the Milchester Prize Brass Band had offered its services free of charge; good-natured Mrs Hallam, the housekeeper at Beechacres, had recruited a willing band of workers to help her with the tea-urns; Roger and Mr Cameron had arranged sports; Miss Marsden and Sister Jones had staged a Handicraft Exhibition of the many lovely articles the little patients had made in Miss Marsden's class; there were flowers and vegetables on sale from the gardens, and a big marquee had been hired. There was even to be a small marquee for soft drinks and ice-cream, so that all that was required was a beautiful day – and now the B.B.C. had promised that too.

' "Everything's coming our way",' Roger chanted blissfully.

'Switch off the radio, Dan, please. There won't be time to listen to the news this morning. There's so much to do over at Beechacres in preparation for tomorrow,' Miss Marsden said.

'It's lucky we got the sports ground all marked and roped off last night. What have you got for us to do this morning, Marsdie?' Roger asked.

'Well, Roger, actually nothing very much for you boys until evening when the men are coming to put up the marquee and will be wanting some assistance; but *I* must get busy arranging the Handwork Exhibition along with Sister Jones.'

'You're not putting the Exhibition outside, are you, Marsdie?' Ruth asked.

'Good gracious, no! It might get caught in one of those occasional showers the B.B.C. so kindly send us. No, we're fixing it up in the Play-room at Beechacres, and we're going to charge a shilling admission and make a lot of money for the St Jonathan's Picnic Fund.'

'I think that's a far better idea,' Susan approved. 'May I sit at the door tomorrow and collect the shillings?'

'Certainly, Susan,' Miss Marsden promised.

'I'm going to help Mrs Hallam with the tea-urns,' Ruth said. 'I'm so glad you persuaded her to let a catering firm provide the buns and cakes, or she'd have worked herself to death.'

'As Mrs Hallam's wise mother would have said, "It's that last iced bun that knocked the nail in mi coffin",' Roger pretended to quote.

Everyone laughed, for Mrs Hallam was always quoting her wise mother, whose sayings had become proverbial. The Brydon's secretly suspected that Mrs Hallam herself was responsible for many of these oracular utterances but, to lend them more weight, she ascribed them to her mother, who appeared to have been possessed of all the wisdom of Solomon, combined with a large dash of Lancashire humour.

Just then a knock was heard at the door.

'I'll go,' Simon volunteered. 'It'll probably be the postman.'

But it wasn't the postman. There on the doorstep stood Mr Cameron, who had given Beechacres to be the Convalescent Hospital and who looked upon all the St Jonathan's Children as his own especial family. In his hand he carried a letter.

'Hallo, Simon. Has Miss Marsden finished her breakfast?' he asked in a rather worried voice.

'Just sitting over my last cup of tea. Do come in and join us, Mr Cameron,' Marsdie invited him. 'You are out and

9

about early this morning. Pour Mr Cameron a cup of tea, please, Ruth.'

Mr Cameron sat down at the breakfast table.

'I've had some rather disquieting news by this morning's post,' he announced. 'I thought I'd better come over and consult you without delay. It's from Mr Bryce, the man in Preston from whom we were hiring crockery for the Garden Party.'

'Oh dear! Don't say he can't supply it? Not at the eleventh hour!' Miss Marsden exclaimed.

'Oh, he can supply it all right, but he can't *deliver* it. He says we'll have to supply our own transport.'

Miss Marsden breathed a sigh of relief. 'If that's the worst, then that's soon remedied. I suppose you'd like me to take the estate car and fetch the crockery?'

'That rather was the idea,' Mr Cameron confessed with a smile. 'But I hesitated to ask, because I know you have so many other irons in the fire today.'

'Oh, we'll take them in our stride,' Marsdie said, gaily mixing her metaphors. 'Cups and saucers and plates we must have, or how shall we feed all our visitors tomorrow? And we'd better have them here as soon as we can, for Mrs Hallam is very pernickety and she's sure to want to wash them all over again, even if they're quite shining already.'

'Yes, she's got a notion that nobody ever washes up properly, except the folk at Beechacres,' Ruth chuckled. 'You'd better get away as soon as you can, Marsdie.'

'I think I'll come with you too, if you'll take me, Miss Marsden,' Mr Cameron suggested. 'There are one or two other final arrangements I want to make in Preston, including the insurance of the marquee, and paying for the printing of the programmes. Perhaps I might be some help, too, in checking the crockery and helping you to stack it in the estate car?'

'You certainly would.'

'All this is going to take some time. I think we'd better agree to lunch in Preston, Miss Marsden, if you've no objection.'

Miss Marsden beamed like a schoolgirl. 'If there's one thing I love, it's my lunch in a café, when I haven't had to plan and shop and cook it all. It will be real fun. Oh, but I forgot –' Miss Marsden's face fell a little. 'What about all the chores there are to do here? The washing-up and the cooking? What about your dinner, *mes enfants*?'

'Now, don't you worry about that,' Ruth advised her. 'We'll see to things here, Marsdie. You and Mr Cameron get away as quickly as you can, and enjoy your lunch.'

Marsdie hesitated. 'Well, if the boys will help with the washing-up and everything –'

'You can leave all that to us, Marsdie,' Roger promised largely.

'That's very nice of you all. Right, then, I'll hurry and get ready now, Mr Cameron.'

'Very well, I'll wait for you,' Mr Cameron said, taking out his pipe.

Miss Marsden ran upstairs, and Ruth began to stack the breakfast dishes on a tray. She was so absorbed in her task that she almost missed Dan sidling to the door – almost, but not quite.

'And where are *you* going, Dan Brydon?' she demanded.

'I'll be back, soon, Ruth,' Dan temporized, his hand still on the latch.

'But *where* are you going?' Ruth persisted.

'Oh, just to fetch Sam Mitton along to lend us a hand too.'

'Oh, no, Dan Brydon, you don't!' Ruth declared, the glint of battle in her eye. 'Not until the washing-up is done.'

'It wouldn't take Dan long to fetch Sam Mitton,' Roger put in, a persuasive voice on Dan's behalf.

'That's all *you* think, Roger,' Ruth told him. 'When Dan gets there, he'll have a second breakfast with Sam – where they put it, I don't know – and then they'll escort each other on a few errands for Mrs Mitton; and before Dan realizes what the time is, the dinner-hour will have come. No, he must stay here and do his share of the house-work.'

Dan sniffed a little in dudgeon. 'Well, it's nice to feel one's *indispensive*,' he remarked.

' "Indispensable", you mean, Dan, you little owl!' Roger chuckled.

Dan was always trying to use long words that he had not properly grasped.

'It means the same thing, anyway,' Dan countered. 'And besides, Sam's bound to come to look for me when I don't turn up there.'

'Too true – I knew it!' Ruth declared. 'Here comes Marsdie. What, ready so soon, Marsdie?'

Miss Marsden, however, was still dressed much as she had been when she went upstairs, in the print overalls she wore for housework.

'Oh, Ruth, I can't find my purse. I think I had it some-where in the kitchen yesterday,' she exclaimed in a rather agitated manner.

'That's all right, Miss Marsden, you won't need it. I've got plenty of money with me.' Mr Cameron said.

'Oh, it's not the money I'm worrying about. It's the garage key and the key of the car. I keep them both in my purse. Unless I find them we can't get the car out.'

'Dear me! That is a more serious matter,' Mr Cameron agreed.

'We'll hunt for it,' Ruth offered. 'You finish off getting ready.'

The Brydons set about a rapid and intensive, search. They were used to hunting for articles Miss Marsden invariably mislaid at the most inopportune moments. Ruth hurriedly scanned the contents of the sideboard drawers.

'Not in here,' she announced.

Simon already had his head inside the kitchen cupboard. 'There's nothing here, not even in the sauce-boat,' he reported. 'The trouble is, you never know in what spot Marsdie's likely to park her purse next.'

'In the tea-caddy?' Dan said hopefully, reaching out a hand to the mantelpiece.

'Mercy me, my lad, you don't really think Marsdie would have put it in the tea-caddy, do you?' Roger asked.

'Things have turned up in the tea-caddy before now,' Dan reminded him darkly. 'Remember that telegram that Mother sent once?'

'But that was just a joke on Marsdie's part.' Ruth generally stood up for Miss Marsden.

Susan was shaking up the cushions on the old settle. 'It's not here either. I wonder what Marsdie was doing when she had her purse last?'

'Probably cooking. Heavens! She *did* make a suet pudding yesterday,' Simon exclaimed with an alarmed expression. 'Things have turned up in puddings too, before now.'

'Cheer up, Simon, we ate the suet pudding yesterday,' Ruth reminded him. 'All the same, I wonder what Marsdie *was* doing? Marsdie, what did you use your purse for yesterday?' she called upstairs.

'Let me think.' Marsdie sounded rather distracted, then announced triumphantly: 'I know! I had it to pay the coalman.'

Roger groaned. 'Suffering cats! Don't say we've got to turn out the coal-cellar now. Oh!'

'Better start with the coal-scuttle,' Simon said practically, poking among its inky depths with the tongs. 'No – no purse. Only one or two pieces of coal.'

'And there's nothing in the vases on the mantelpiece, nor behind the clock,' Roger said, making an investigation.

'Have you looked *in* the clock?' Simon asked. 'Marsdie might have been winding it up when the coalman called.'

'Hi, Marsdie, what were you doing when the coalman did call?' Roger cried up the stairs in his turn.

'I was scrubbing the kitchen table after preparing the dinner,' Marsdie replied.

Dan flew to the wash-house for the bucket. 'The purse isn't here. Do you think she can have poured it away down the drain with the dirty water?' he asked quite seriously.

'Marsdie's purse is quite a big one, and there happens to be a grating over the drain,' Roger laughed; but all the same he went and inspected the grating. No use taking any chances when Marsdie had lost something!

'What else did you do yesterday, Miss Marsden?' Mr Cameron wanted to know.

Miss Marsden appeared at the head of the stairs in the act of donning her coat. 'Let me see: I swept and dusted and got some of St Jonathan's handwork ready for the Exhibition. Oh, yes, and I patched the seat of Dan's trousers.'

Ruth dashed at the duster drawer, while Susan investigated the contents of Miss Marsden's suitcase in which she kept her handwork materials. Dan felt gingerly at the seat of his shorts.

'Marsdie hasn't sewn the purse in, or I'd have been sitting on a lump,' he announced.

The situation was growing desperate when Simon gave a cry of triumph. 'Here it is! *Inside* the sewing-machine cover.'

'How did you think of that spot, Simon?' Ruth said with relief.

'Dan's patch. It's machined on, not handsewn. Therefore Marsdie must have had the machine out yesterday and the chances were that she popped the purse down on the machine table. So she did, under the cover. Elementary, my dear Watson.'

'The purse is found, Miss Marsden,' Mr Cameron called up the stairs.

'How lucky! I'm just ready.' Miss Marsden ran down the stairs, jabbing a hat-pin in place as she ran. 'Bless you all for finding it! Yes, the keys are in it all right. We can go now, Mr Cameron. Good-bye, *mes enfants*.' She was almost through the door when she exclaimed: 'Oh dear, where's my handbag now?'

'Under your arm, Marsdie,' Ruth said patiently.

'Oh, yes, so it is. We'll be back as soon as we can. Enjoy your dinner, my dears, as much as I'm going to enjoy mine! Bye-bye.'

The door closed behind Miss Marsden and Mr Cameron.

'*Whew!*' Roger whistled, pretending to mop his brow. 'She's off at last; but I began to think we were going to have to break open the door of the garage.'

'I'm almost dizzy with hunting about,' Ruth admitted. 'What a dash round we've had! All the same, I'm glad we found the purse, for Marsdie would have worried all the time if we hadn't, and I want her to enjoy her outing. She's such a dear and does so much for us. But now to work. We'll clear the table and wash up first.'

'I say, what's the hurry?' Roger grumbled.

'If we don't start promptly we shall be behind-hand all day. You boys have no idea what there is to do in a house. You think if the washing-up's done and the dinner cooked, all we have to do is to sit back and get out our knitting.'

'Well, isn't it?' Roger asked impudently.

'My word, if you had everything to do, you'd whistle a different tune!' Ruth retorted severely. 'I think Marsdie's wonderful the way she gets through everything so cheerfully, even though we do try to lend her a hand.'

'Oh, I grant Marsdie's wonderful,' Roger agreed readily. 'Well, let's be having the list of tasks to be done. What do you expect from us boys?'

Ruth considered. 'Well, after washing the dishes, you can each make your own beds and then peel the potatoes and prepare the vegetables, then chop sticks for tomorrow's fire, and then the tables and the kitchen and the bathroom should be scrubbed, too –'

Ruth paused for lack of breath. During this recital, Roger's face had been growing longer and longer.

'I say, where do you and Susan come in on all this?' he wanted to know.

'You don't need to *eat*, by any chance?' Ruth inquired with sarcasm. 'We've got all the cooking to do, and there are the bedrooms to sweep and dust, and it's the day to go shopping to bring the groceries and meat from Milchester.'

'Couldn't Dan fetch the groceries?'

'Do you think I'd trust Dan to choose meat and fish?' Ruth exclaimed. 'He'd be back with it about supper time, if he happened to meet Sam Mitton. That reminds me, Roger –' Ruth clapped her hand to her head: 'My bicycle's got a puncture. If I'm to go shopping in Milchester, I'll need it mending right now, please.'

Roger dropped the dish-towel he was preparing to use. Ruth was quite evidently in one of what Dan called her 'bossy moods', which sprang from her gift for energetic organization; but for once Roger was annoyed.

'If that's not the limit!' he exclaimed. 'I've not only to be housemaid but handy-man as well. Why didn't you tell me about it yesterday? You must have known you had a puncture then. I could have done it easily enough last night, but today I want to tidy up the garden ready for the Garden Party.'

Ruth was instantly on her high horse. 'I've half a mind to mend it myself,' she declared.

All might have been well if Roger had kept a still tongue in his head and been able to resist the gibe. 'Do you know how?'

'Of course I do!' Ruth exploded. 'But if I mend that

puncture, you boys will jolly well have to get your own dinner.'

To her surprise, Roger took her at her word. 'All right, go ahead,' he said calmly.

'That's awfully mean of you, Roger Brydon,' Susan cried, taking up the cudgels on Ruth's behalf. Her twin, Simon, however, did not side with her as usual, but pointed out, 'You know, Susan, I rather think Ruth started the argument.'

'I'm jolly sure she did, with all her horrid *aspirations* about Sam Mitton and me,' Dan chimed in self-righteously.

' "Aspersions", you mean, Dan, you little donkey! Don't try to use big words you don't understand,' Susan snapped at him.

'Great guns! This seems to be resolving itself into a battle of the sexes, with you and Susan against the rest of us,' Roger exclaimed, rather appalled at the suddenness with which this breeze had sprung up when there seemed to have been no cloud on the horizon.

'Yes, and don't forget that Sam Mitton will be here any moment now,' Dan put in, counting another recruit to his side.

'Sam Mitton! Sam's the only one of the lot of you who has any sense,' Ruth declared sweepingly. 'Did you mean what you said about mending my own bike, Roger?' she demanded.

'Sure! Every word of it,' Roger replied stubbornly.

Susan saw, too late, the way things were drifting. 'Oh, Roger, don't be so obstinate! Climb down, and then Ruth will too,' she pleaded, but Ruth tossed her head defiantly.

'Oh, no, I shan't – you'll have to get your own meals now,' she threw out in challenge. Roger took it up forthwith.

'All right, Ruth. But, look here, let's make a competition of it, instead of quarrelling. It *would* be rather fun to swop jobs. We'll do *your* household chores and the cooking, if you'll do our work. That's fair enough, isn't it?' he added in a tone meant to be placatory.

Ruth, however, was not to be so easily mollified. She sniffed.

'It sounds all right, but a pretty mess you'll make of it.'

Roger shrugged his shoulders. 'Oh, there may be a few mistakes made on both sides,' he said airily. 'But we'll take you at your word and show you what we can do, eh, boys?' he appealed to the other two. They stood by him loyally.

'Yes, Roger, we're with you. We're not going to let the girls get away with it.'

'All right, then. We'll change jobs. I'll mend my own puncture and we'll scrub out the kitchen and bathroom and chop sticks. We'll all make our own beds and get through the breakfast washing-up together; but you've to sweep and dust everywhere else, including the bedrooms, and do all the shopping and cooking.' Ruth had begun to draw up the rules.

'And don't forget to buy something tasty for supper,' Susan threw in for good weight. They reckoned without Dan's contribution to Roger's side of the scales, however:

'You'll be careful when you're cleaning out my rabbit hutches, not to let the rabbits loose, won't you, Ruth?' he asked in all seeming innocence.

'Cleaning out your rabbit hutches! That's not in the list of household duties,' Ruth protested indignantly.

'No, but it was my job and Sam's. If we're doing your work, you've got to do ours. It's only fair.'

'It won't take us long, Ruth. It's just that Dan makes such a fuss about it,' Susan said.

'All right. We'll do the rabbit hutches too,' Ruth agreed, with the air of one willing to take on all comers.

'Fresh straw and plenty of greenstuff, mind,' Dan instructed them. 'Ah! Here's Sam Mitton. Hullo, Sam, you're just in time,' Dan hailed his chum with delight.

'What for? Hullo, everybody,' Sam said all in a breath.

'To roll up your sleeves, Sam, and get busy sweeping and dusting,' Ruth told him sweetly, pushing a duster into his hand. 'You boys are doing our work today, and we're to do yours, and see who gets on best. It's a kind of competition with no prizes for the winners.'

'Eh, it sounds proper rum to me, but I'm game,' Sam declared. 'When do we start?'

'Right now. The washing-up is a combined operation, for this meal *only*, as I'd like you boys to get a good start. Even though you're four to two, you'll need it. After the other meals, the washing-up will be your pigeon,' Ruth informed them.

'I don't think the washing-up was mentioned when we drew up the rules,' Roger hedged.

'Neither were the rabbit hutches!' Ruth countered quickly. 'Take it or leave it, the washing-up is on your side of the account.'

'I guess you'd have made *us* help with it, Ruth,' Dan grumbled.

Simon began to dry the knives and forks at terrific speed.

'Oh, let's stop arguing and get on with the job, or at this rate we'll never be finished,' he urged everybody; and, seeing the sense of this argument, they all set to with a will.

CHAPTER TWO

The game of 'Family Coach' begins

As soon as the washing-up was completed and the beds made, Roger began to organize his squad to do the other household tasks which fell to their lot.

'Now, Simon and I will sweep and dust the bedrooms while you and Sam –' he began.

'Rut the errands in Milchester?' Dan put in eagerly – too eagerly, for Roger remembered Ruth's forebodings.

'No. On second thoughts Simon had better go on his bicycle for the meat and groceries, and the rest of us will tackle the bedrooms,' he decided.

'Oh!' Dan exclaimed in a disappointed tone. His little plan had not worked.

'Team work, my lad! Team work!' Roger said briskly. 'I'll take the sweeper and go over the carpets and rugs, and you can use that brush and sweep the linoleum, and Sam can follow us both with a duster and do the furniture.'

'Shouldn't the rugs be shaken?' Simon suggested.

'Totally unnecessary. Not when I've swept them. Women love to do a lot of unnecessary work.'

'What am I to bring from Milchester?' Simon wanted to know.

'Oh, the groceries, and a chunk of meat of some kind for dinner, and any other good thing you may see lying around waiting for someone to adopt it.'

'And something tasty for supper,' Dan added.

'All right, I'll remember,' Simon promised.

'And don't be too long away. It'll be all hands on deck when it comes to cooking the dinner,' Roger told him.

'I should have thought it would be all hands in the galley. Getting a bit mixed, aren't you?' Simon said cheekily, then added, 'All right. I'll be as quick as I can.'

'And now, let's get busy,' Roger said, leading the way upstairs.

He wielded the sweeper with so much vigour that clouds of dust floated out and settled on all the furniture. Dan followed him obediently with the long-haired brush, sweeping all the linoleum borders, until he had collected a neat little pile of dust in one corner.

'I say, Roger, what am I to do with this?' he asked.

Roger scratched his head doubtfully. 'I suppose we ought to take it up on a shovel or something and put it in the dustbin, but that means running up and down the stairs. It can wait till we're ready to go down. Just push it under this mat and then we shall know where to look for it when we've finished.'

'Oh, Dan, look out,' Sam cried suddenly in a warning voice.

As Dan swung round, the handle of the brush caught something on Miss Marsden's dressing table and swept it off. It fell with a thud on to a thick woollen rug.

'Eh, you've gone and knocked Miss Marsden's powder bowl flying,' Sam said in consternation.

'Is it broken?' Roger asked anxiously, rushing to look at it.

Sam picked it up from the rug and examined it closely.

'No, it's all right. Not even chipped, luckily. But look at the powder all over the place, just where you've swept. It's all wasted.'

'You are a careless little clown, Dan. What will Marsdie say?'

'It'll be her birthday soon,' Dan said penitently. 'I'll buy her another box of powder – that's if it's not fearfully expensive,' he added cautiously.

'Just look at this mess,' Roger said in despair, as he surveyed the fine powder dust settling all over the floor and furniture. 'Now we've got to start sweeping all over again.'

Roger swept vigorously for a couple of minutes, then paused to survey the results of his labours.

'It's a queer thing, but the faster I sweep, the more dust seems to rise. At this rate it's going to take us all day to finish the bedrooms.'

Once more the trio set to work with sweeper, brush and duster, and more than ever Dan wished it had fallen to his lot to do the shopping, while Roger began to think that there was more to this cleaning business than met the eye, and Sam plodded steadily and methodically on.

Meanwhile, down in the kitchen, Ruth and Susan had halved the floor scrubbing, and by dint of trying to race each other, had soon wiped the soap off the last square yard and finished in a dead heat. As they wrung out their floor-cloths and emptied their buckets, they congratulated each other on the slick way they had got through a hard task.

'What shall we tackle next? The rabbit hutches? Or

shall we mend that puncture?' Ruth asked in high good spirits.

'Rabbit hutches, I would say,' Susan replied. 'As we haven't to do the shopping, there's no hurry for the bike.'

Just then Roger appeared at the kitchen door, bearing his carpet-sweeper with him. 'Hallo, girls! Getting on?' he asked.

'Now don't tell us you've done the bedrooms already,' Ruth exclaimed in incredulous tones. 'You haven't even brought the rugs down to shake outside.'

'Oh, we're just leaving the dust to settle while we get ahead with another job,' Roger explained airily. 'That's where *method* comes in, you know.'

'Mm! It may sound all right,' Ruth sniffed. 'We've finished our scrubbing and we're off to the rabbit hutches now.'

'Er – before you go – have you peeled the potatoes and prepared the vegetables for dinner? That was on your side of the contract, remember,' Roger grinned at them.

'Oh, bother you, Roger! There'll be plenty of time when we've finished the hutches. You get on with the other preparations,' Ruth directed him.

'Yes, don't forget that you've got a pudding to make,' Susan fired at him in her turn. 'We'll be back in about fifteen minutes. Good-bye.'

When they had gone, Roger rubbed his hands gleefully.

'I thought that would hurry them out,' he said to himself. 'Now I've got the kitchen all to myself.'

He hunted through the bookshelf below the cupboard.

'Where's Marsdie's old cookery book? Ah, here it is. Now, let's see what there is to this cookery business that all these women make so much fuss about.'

As he was busy turning the pages, Simon came in, rather breathless, for he had cycled fast from the village.

'Hallo, Roger – here are the food supplies. What are you doing with that cookery book?'

'Trying to decide what kind of a pudding to make. You wouldn't think there were so many different varieties to choose from, would you?' he remarked, rapidly scanning the pages.

'Hadn't you better choose something simple, like semolina?' Simon cautiously advised. Roger, however, despised such a prosaic idea.

'Semolina, my foot! This is going to be a real slap-up dinner, my lad, where we fairly put it across the girls. Oh, yes, we're going in for something a bit more ambitious than semolina. By the way, what kind of meat did you get, Simon?'

Simon began to unwrap the package in his carrier-basket.

'It's brisket of beef, so the butcher said,' he explained a little doubtfully.

Roger surveyed this rather strange-looking piece of meat and prodded it gently with his forefinger.

'Mm! Something like sausages might have been a bit simpler to begin with,' he said thoughtfully.

'I thought you said you wanted to do something ambitious,' Simon reminded him. 'Anyway, the butcher had no sausages.'

'Well, we'll do something with the meat that's a bit out

of the ordinary,' Roger promised. 'Oh, did you remember to bring something a bit tasty for supper?'

Simon looked slightly crestfallen. 'All I could get were some kippers.'

Roger looked a little dubiously at the highly-coloured specimens Simon produced from his basket.

'Not very original, but I suppose if there was nothing else –'

Simon took this criticism of his shopping activities in very poor part. 'You're jolly lucky to get these kippers,' he snapped. 'I tell you, I almost snatched these from under Mrs Entwhistle's nose. Shopping isn't so easy as all that. That's one thing Ruth was right about.'

'Oh, all right – but don't tell her so,' Roger cautioned him. 'And now about this pudding. Let's see: apple dumpling – apple pudding –' he flicked the leaves of the cookery book over rapidly. 'Bachelor pudding – that sounds very suitable.' He paused.

'Read on, Roger. Let's hear what else there is,' Simon begged.

'Batter pudding – no. Bread pudding – rather stodgy.'

'That's the kind of thing Ruth makes when she can't think of anything else,' Dan commented. He and Sam had decided that there was no more credit to be had by bedroom cleaning, and had joined Roger and Simon in the kitchen just as Roger proceeded to the selection of his menu.

'Canary pudding!' Roger said hopefully, rather intrigued with the title. 'Bother! There's a bit torn out of the cookery book there. Exeter pudding? "Take three eggs," ' he began to read.

'Aren't three eggs rather a lot?' Simon asked doubtfully. 'Besides, I heard Ruth say that the eggs would be needed for breakfast.'

'I'm making this pudding, not Ruth,' Roger reminded him a little tartly; then he continued to mumble over the list of ingredients half to himself. 'Sponge cakes, suet, sugar, two or three tablespoons of cream, grated lemon rind, jam sauce —'

'Eh, Roger, it sounds proper rich,' Sam Mitton interpolated.

'A wineglass of sherry or rum, optional . . .' Roger came to an abrupt conclusion. 'I'm afraid that's torn it,' he lamented. 'We haven't got any sherry or rum.'

'Couldn't you use a glass of optional instead?' Dan asked.

'Dan, you little donkey, "optional" means you can please yourself about it.'

'Then what are you worrying about?' Dan inquired with perfect logic.

'Probably if we leave it out it's just one of those things which would spoil the whole dish. No, we'll look for something else,' Roger decided.

'What about a 'Asty pudding? My mother allus makes a 'Asty pudding on washing days,' Sam Mitton made his contribution to the debate.

'A what?' Roger asked, puzzled.

'A 'Asty pudding. "'Asty" because it's quick, you know. It only takes about a quarter of an hour.'

'Oh, I see. A Hasty pudding. But we've got lots of time yet,' Roger said easily.

'You won't have, if you don't make up your mind soon what you'll do,' Simon warned him.

'Here's one that sounds all right,' Roger said, pouncing

on the book again. '*Paradise* pudding. Yes, Paradise pudding it shall be. You take four ounces of coarsely chopped apples – we've plenty of apples – four ounces of sugar – four ounces of currants or sultanas –'

'There aren't any currants. I heard Marsdie say so,' Simon told him.

'Then it'll have to be the sultanas.' Roger read rapidly on. ' "Four ounces of bread-crumbs. Two eggs." '

'Two eggs,' Simon repeated, wrinkling his brows. 'Well, I daresay we can get some more from the farm.'

'That's a thought,' Roger conceded. ' "Rind of half a lemon – nut of butter – salt – nutmeg –" Mm! It sounds quite simple. "Serve with a fruit or jam sauce." Yes, I think we could manage that. Let's all start in now. You can chop the apples, Dan. Simon, you hunt up the other things. Sam, can you see to the bread-crumbs while I beat up the eggs?'

Soon they were all busily at work. Roger rubbed his hands gleefully.

'This is team work, this is. We'll show Ruth,' he declared with enthusiasm.

Dan, however, was looking at the couple of large apples in a puzzled way. 'Do I have to peel the apples first?' he asked reluctantly.

Roger seized the cookery book again. 'Let's look at the recipe. All it says is "Chop the apples coarsely". It doesn't say a word about peeling them first. Go ahead with the chopping, Dan.'

Roger was beating away manfully at the eggs with a fork.

'Gee! How my wrist aches!' he declared, 'and the yolk and the white are still streaky!'

Sam also was looking rather mournfully at the bread. 'This loaf won't turn into crumbs very well. It looks rather new and soft.'

'Oh, just stick it through the mincer,' Roger directed him.

Sam got to work to fit the mincer together and to feed the bread into it.

Simon looked up from his task, knife in hand. 'Did you say a *nut* of butter?'

'Yes.'

'What size of nut? Monkey nut or coconut?'

This was a poser indeed, and Roger referred once more to the cookery book, but again he got no enlightenment.

'This book doesn't say. The term's a bit elastic, isn't it? Somewhere between the two, I should say, Simon. Cut off a hunk, about half that slab.'

'This is margarine,' Simon explained. 'Ruth would just about blow up altogether if we used all the butter.'

'The pudding won't taste quite so good, but we'll have to put up with that,' Roger said regretfully. 'Ruth's touchy enough today, as it is.'

'Add the rind of half a lemon,' Simon quoted in his turn from the book.

'Just peel the lemon half-way round. That should do. How are the bread crumbs doing, Sam?'

'They're coming out in long grey kind of worms, not a bit like bread crumbs,' Sam said dubiously.

'I daresay they'll taste just the same when they're mixed with the other ingredients. Here's the mixing bowl. Now, each of you pitch your ingredients in and I'll stir the lot up,' Roger directed.

'How much salt?' Simon asked.

'The recipe says "Salt to taste". I suppose that means we've got to be able to taste it fairly well. What about a couple of tablespoons?'

Obediently Simon measured out two tablespoons of salt and tipped them into the mixture.

'Now, what about the nutmeg?' he asked.

'Marsdie keeps them in a tin on the second shelf of the store-cupboard,' Dan said.

'Yes, here it is. I say, Roger, shouldn't we grind it up or something?'

'All the recipe says is "Nutmeg" – just plain "Nutmeg." We'll drop it in and maybe it'll dissolve, as sugar does, while the pudding's cooking. Everything in now? Then we'll all give it a stir round for luck and then turn it into this basin.'

They followed Roger's instructions, then Dan asked what was next to be done with the pudding. Simon referred to the cookery book again, now grown sticky with much handling.

'It says, "Steam for three hours",' He cast an apprehensive glance at the clock. 'What are we to do about it, Roger? It's only an hour to dinner time.'

'Oh, that's all nonsense,' Roger said breezily. 'These old-fashioned cookery books always spent *hours* over things. If we stick the basin straight into boiling water and keep it boiling fast, it'll cook just as well. And now for that meat. Just look up "Brisket" in that cookery book, Simon, while I put the pudding on to boil.'

Simon ran his finger down the index and turned to the appropriate page. He paused for a moment, then gave a dismayed exclamation.

'Oh, Roger, we ought to rub the meat over with vinegar

and let it stand three hours before cooking.'

'What good will that do? Who wants meat tasting of vinegar? Besides, we want it for dinner *today*. Skip that bit and go on to the next.'

' "Put it in a stew-pan just large enough to hold it and barely cover the brisket with water. Bring to the boil and simmer gently for about an hour." '

Roger appeared more relieved. 'That's simple enough, and it should be done just in time for dinner.'

Simon soon dashed his hopes to the ground. 'Oh, but that's not all of it. At the end of an hour you add the prepared vegetables and a – a *"bouquet garni"* – whatever that may be, and you simmer for a further two-and-a-half hours.' Simon's eyes were big with consternation as he read the last passage.

'If we listened to all that book says, we'd be having dinner at supper time,' Roger rejoined testily. 'I guess it was written by some silly woman who wanted to make out that this cooking business is an overtime job instead of a spare-time occupation. If that chunk of meat boils for an hour, *fast*, like the pudding, you'll see, it'll be done to a turn.'

Feeling certain that he knew far better than Marsdie's old-fashioned cookery book, Roger set to work with all the assurance of an experienced chef of a continental hotel.

*   *   *

Down in the garden at Beechacres Susan and Ruth were busily engaged in preparing a meal for Dan's numerous families of rabbits. They seemed to require mountainous quantities of food.

'There's the bran-mash and the cabbage leaves and

other green stuff. I hope we've got enough for them now. You'd never think it would take so long to search for dandelions, would you?' Ruth appealed to Susan. 'I don't know why Dan wants to keep so many rabbits.'

'He usually cleans out the hutches before he gives the rabbits their food,' Susan said.

'Then we'd better do the same. Will you fetch some straw from the shed, please, Susan?'

While Susan was gone to fetch the straw, Ruth set about the business of cleaning the hutches. As she worked she hummed a little careless tune to herself. She opened wide the door of one hutch to rake out the old straw, entirely regardless of the warning Dan had given her against letting the rabbits loose. Peter the Giant peeped from his inner sleeping compartment and watched the movements of the rake. Cunningly he awaited his opportunity – the moment when Ruth's back would be turned and the door of the hutch still open. Like lightning he snatched the opportunity when it did occur and with a bound he was out of the hutch and among the cabbages in Roger's garden. Ruth dropped the rake and went after him, heedless that she had left the door of yet another hutch swinging on its hinges.

'Come back, Peter! Come back, you bad bunny! Oh dear! Oh, Susan!'

'What's the matter?' Susan asked, appearing just then with an armful of straw.

'Dan's prize rabbit's got loose. Oh, and there goes another! It's Bucking Billy, the new one. Susan, do drop that heap of straw and help me to chase them in again.'

Susan did as Ruth wished, and both girls were soon scampering breathlessly after the two wicked rabbits, who, with a bob of their white tails and a twisting kick of their hind legs, darted from their reach every time the girls were about to grasp them.

'Oh, there's Peter among Roger's cauliflowers now. He's nibbling at the one Roger meant for the Milchester show. Roger will be mad.'

Ruth made even more frenzied attempts to lay hold of the rabbit, while Susan did her best to snatch Bucking Billy from among the young lettuces.

'Got him!' Susan cried triumphantly, but she rejoiced too soon, for, with a sideways kick and twist of his ears, Bucking Billy was free again and had begun to play Ring-o'-Roses with Susan round an apple tree.

'There's no stalking this rabbit,' Ruth cried in desperation. 'As soon as you think you're within grabbing distance, he winks one eye and twitches one ear and then he's off again. It's hopeless.'

'Oh dear! We'll never get them back to the hutches again,' Susan wailed.

Just then a welcome voice greeted them, and the flaming carroty head of Charlie Carter came round the doorway in the wall between the vegetable and flower gardens at Beechacres. Charlie was one of the oldest patients in St Jonathan's. His 'game leg', as he called it, had been in plaster for a long time, but now he was practically cured and as strong as ever, and he hoped soon to go to Sam Mitton's aunt's farm at Stainfold to learn farming. He chuckled as he watched the girls' frantic efforts to retrieve the rabbits.

'Oh, Charlie, thank goodness you've come to help us,' Ruth cried.

'Whatever shall we do?' Susan asked breathlessly.

'Prop the doors of their hutches open and put a dish of that bran-mash inside each hutch.'

The girls hastened to obey Charlie's instructions.

'Now, chivvy 'em up easy-like towards the hutches. Don't startle them or they'll gallop round like mad. Just work 'em a foot or two at a time in the right direction.'

'Are we doing all right?' Susan asked anxiously as they edged the rabbits nearer to the hutches.

'Champion! That's the way,' Charlie applauded. 'They're near enough to the hutches now to get the scent of the bran-mash. Now, just leave 'em alone, but stand still between them and the garden and if they make a move in that direction turn 'em back again very quietly to the hutches. The thing is not to get them mad.'

Gently, but deliberately, Ruth and Susan forced the two rabbits nearer and nearer to their homes. Once Peter stopped and sat up on his hind-legs, twitching his nose and whiskers. Then he lolloped easily towards the saucer of bran-mash and with forepaws resting on the floor of the hutch, he sniffed at the bran-mash and then began to nibble at it.

'This is where I do *my* stuff,' Charlie whispered, and, tiptoeing up behind the rabbit so as not to scare him, gave him a gentle little tap on the rump which startled the rabbit enough to make him take a jump in the right direction – into the hutch. Quick as lightning Charlie slammed shut the hutch door and bolted it.

'Aye, he's a crafty one, is Peter, but he's safe home again,' he grinned with satisfaction.

Ruth was watching the antics of the other rabbit anxiously. Once Charlie had moved away from the hutches again, Bucking Billy approached, sniffed, like

35

Peter, at his food, and then entered the hutch of his own accord.

'Just look at that, after all our wild running about,' Ruth exclaimed.

'Yes, these little animals know their own hutches right enough. I daresay, if we left them alone, they'd hop in and out all day, and if it wasn't for the vegetable garden, they could. Have they done much damage?'

'No. Thanks to your coming along so promptly, Charlie, they didn't have much chance,' Ruth said gratefully.

'Yes, thanks an awful lot,' Susan added.

'You're welcome. Glad to oblige,' Charlie replied a little awkwardly, rather embarrassed at being thanked. 'Where's Dan that he's not looking after his own rabbits?' he asked, to change the subject.

'Oh, he's busy with something in the house, so we're doing this for him. Oh, Susan, where's that bundle of straw you put down when you tried to catch the rabbits?' Ruth asked suddenly.

It was only too evident what had happened. The gusts of wind which kept sweeping the garden had disintegrated the bundle of straw which was blowing in wisps all over the garden, clinging here and there to the vegetables and fruit bushes.

'Oh, what a mess!' Susan sighed.

'Now we'll have to go round picking up bits of straw,' Ruth grumbled in exasperation. 'We can't leave the garden in this untidy condition.'

Again Charlie Carter came to the rescue. 'There are a couple of rakes in the tool-shed and a long hoe. It won't take long if we all three get busy.'

'Bless you, Charlie Carter!' Ruth said fervently. ' "A bit of help is worth a deal of pity", as somebody – not Mrs Hallam's wise mother – certainly said.'

Once more they all set to work with a will.

CHAPTER THREE

Punctures and Paradise pudding

'THERE are your vegetables, Roger. What an awful lot you wanted. And that huge panful of potatoes, too! You must think we've all got tremendous appetites.'

Ruth set down on the kitchen table the big bowl full of mixed vegetables that she and Susan had been preparing.

'Perhaps the boys want to make sure of something eatable for dinner,' Susan said slyly.

'Don't be waspish, Susan, even if you don't like peeling potatoes,' Roger replied quickly. 'Smell that good smell, eh?' He jerked his head in the direction of the cooking stove.

'There's certainly a good smell,' Ruth agreed. 'It's a bit like hot cake.'

'That's the pudding cooking,' Roger said with conscious pride.

'What kind of pudding?' Susan questioned him inquisitively.

'Paradise pudding,' Roger informed her.

'Never heard of it!' Ruth sniffed.

'Oh, you've a lot to learn yet, Ruth,' Roger told her patronizingly.

'Perhaps the proof of the pudding –' Ruth began to

hint. 'By the way – have you had time to do your knitting yet, Roger?' she teased him.

'Oh, scoot! Go and mend your bike,' Roger retorted.

'Right! We will. Call us when dinner's ready,' Ruth said, with just a touch of mockery in her voice.

She and Susan found the repair outfit, got a bucket of water, and brought the bicycle out on to the garden path.

'I think Roger usually turns the bicycle upside down,' Ruth said.

'Yes,' Susan agreed. Together they turned the bicycle in rather unwieldy fashion on to its handlebars.

'The next thing is to get the outer tyre off,' Susan said.

'I wonder which tool Roger uses for that?' Ruth inquired.

'One of these tools in the kitbag, but I don't know which,' Susan confessed.

'There's Sam going along with something to the dustbin. Let's ask him. He won't give us away to Roger.'

'Sst! Sam!' Susan made a hissing noise through her teeth to attract Sam's attention.

Sam stopped in the act of lifting the dustbin lid and looked at them inquiringly.

'Which tool do we use to take the tyre off?' Susan asked him in a sepulchral whisper.

'Try the spanner,' Sam replied in something of the manner of a ventriloquist who does not wish to be detected in speech.

Ruth signalled her thanks in pantomime and hunted afresh in the kit-bag.

'Here it is, Susan. I suppose we adjust the spanner to the size of the tyre and lift.'

Ruth carefully screwed the spanner to the desired space, then attacked the tyre with it.

'Bother!' she exclaimed, after struggling unsuccessfully with it for a minute or two. 'Bother! If it's slack it just slips off the tyre and when I tighten it up, it just grips and nothing happens.'

She looked up to find Sam grinning at their efforts.

'Eh, Ruth, what are you up to? Try t'other end of the spanner,' he chuckled.

'What! The handle?' Ruth exclaimed, astounded.

'Aye. It's curved at the end to make a kind of lever. You push it under the tyre and lift.'

'Oh, I see,' Ruth said a little uncertainly.

'If you don't say anything to Roger, I could have that tyre off in a couple of shakes,' Sam said, eyeing the bicycle wistfully. There was nothing Sam enjoyed more than tinkering with a bicycle.

'It's nice of you, Sam, but we'll play fair,' Ruth answered firmly. 'Besides, we'd rather like to try puncture-mending for ourselves. You run along and do your job. By the way, what are you doing?' she asked curiously.

'Setting the table for dinner,' Sam told her gloomily. 'I hope I break nowt.'

'Is it near dinner time already?' Ruth said in surprise. 'Goodness, Susan, if we're to have this thing done before dinner, we'll have to be smart. Give me a hand to lever this top tyre off, will you?'

Together they worked with the lever.

'It's coming now. You've got one edge over the rim of the wheel. Good! It's off,' Susan cried with satisfaction.

'What next?' Ruth asked, looking in bewilderment at the snaky inner tube of the tyre, now flat and deflated.

'We take the inner tube and run it through this bucket of water and watch for bubbles,' Susan told her.

Twice they passed the tyre through the water without the sign of a bubble coming up.

'Look! There's Sam grinning at us through the kitchen window,' Susan said.

Sam was laughing at them and making a vigorous pantomime to indicate the pumping of air into the tyre, but neither Ruth nor Susan could understand what he meant. He raised the kitchen window very cautiously.

'Try blowing up the tyre first,' he advised them. 'The bubbles of air won't come out if there's no air in t' tube, I reckon.'

'How stupid of us! Hand me the bicycle pump, please, Susan.'

Ruth pumped vigorously at the tyre until it was swollen, then she slipped it through the water in the bucket again. This time bubbles of air certainly came to the surface. Susan slipped her thumb over the hole in the tyre.

'That's the spot. What now?'

'Let's see what it says on the repair outfit,' Ruth suggested. 'Thoroughly clean tube with sandpaper,' she read.

She rubbed vigorously at the tube with the rough paper until Susan cautioned her not to rub the tyre into a hole.

'Now, what?' Ruth said, reading the directions again. ' "Coat the tube only with the adhesive solution".'

Ruth applied the sticky gum in rather a wholesale fashion. It lay thick and glistening on the inner tube.

'Haven't you put rather a lot on?' Susan asked.

'Oh, that will help the patch to adhere better,' Ruth said with confidence. 'Now to put the patch on.'

She pressed it down into the miniature sea of gummy solution and it oozed thickly all round the edges of the patch.

'Oh, bother! The patch keeps curling up.'

'I knew you'd used too much solution. Try wiping a bit off,' Susan advised.

Ruth applied a corner of a duster and wiped off the surplus solution. 'Yes. That's better. The patch is sticking now,' she announced with satisfaction. 'After all, that was very simple. All we've got to do is to fix on the tyre again.'

Susan slipped the valve through the hole in the wheel rim and together they rolled the inner tube into place by revolving the wheel gently. The stiff outside tyre, however, proved a far more difficult task. Together they struggled with it for several minutes.

'It's a bit tiresome, isn't it?' Susan said, somewhat out of breath. 'As fast as you get one bit on the rim, another bit slips off.'

'I – just – can't – get – this side – over the rim – at all,' panted Ruth.

'Keep on, Ruth. Keep on. It's coming.' Susan encouraged her.

'It's on. Hurrah!' Ruth cried, as at last the tyre slipped into place; but her triumph was short-lived, for when she revolved the wheel to inspect the tyre, there was a big piece of the inner tube nipped between the outer tyre and the rim.

'Oh, bother it!' Ruth almost wept with annoyance. 'I

suppose that means we'll have to take the tyre off all over again. Of all the exasperating things! I am sick of it.'

'So am I!' Susan declared, looking and feeling very hot. She picked up the spanner again and levered once more at the tyre.

'You'd think the thing was bewitched,' Ruth said, pulling feverishly at her side. 'Well, at least we can get the thing *off*!'

'Oh, but look!' Susan cried, consternation in her voice. 'There's a slit in the inner tube now, just close to where the puncture was before. It's about an inch long.'

Ruth bent over the tyre only to find Susan's statement was too true.

'How on earth did that come there?' she exclaimed, utterly mystified.

There was a tap again on the kitchen window and there was Sam Mitton making signs at them. He looked round carefully first to make sure Roger was not listening before he proffered further advice.

'Did you look the outer tyre over for the thing which caused the first puncture?' he whispered.

'The thing that caused the first puncture? What do you mean?' Ruth whispered back in her turn.

'' 'Appen there's a nail or a thorn still sticking in the tyre. Look inside at the lining.'

Susan scrutinized the tyre closely. 'Here! There's a tin-tack still sticking in the tyre. That's what ripped it the second time.'

Suddenly Roger called from the scullery, 'Look alive with setting that table, Sam. I shall want a hand with dishing up the dinner,' and Sam disappeared like a rabbit into a burrow.

'Now we've got to start all over again. Where's that tube of solution? Where *is* that tube of solution?' Ruth cried, growing more exasperated every moment. Susan began to hunt round, too.

'Oh dear! You're standing on it, Ruth, and the cap's come off. There's a long sticky worm of gummy solution all over the garden path.'

'Oh, my! This is the limit,' Ruth declared, at the point of despair.

Just then a hail came from the kitchen. 'Come in, girls, the dinner's ready.' It was Roger calling.

Ruth made a desperate attempt to apply another patch but it fell off again.

'I think we'll just have to leave this puncture for a while, Susan. Perhaps when we're fresher after dinner, we can tackle it better.'

'We'll just leave the inner tube hanging out, ready to start work again afterwards, shall we?'

'All right. I'm just disgusted with it,' Ruth said.

'Are you girls coming? Everything's getting cold,' Roger called again.

'All right. Do give us time to wash our hands,' Ruth cried, scrubbing away at the dirt and oil upon her fingers.

'Pull out the chairs for the girls, Dan. Simon, you serve the vegetables, while I carve the meat.' Roger gave his directions with the air of the perfect host.

'I say, you girls do look hot,' Simon commented.

'So would you, if –' Susan began, but Ruth silenced her with a look.

Roger was beginning to hack at the joint in a rather doggedly determined fashion.

'You seem to be having a bit of trouble with the carving, Roger,' Ruth remarked, anxious to lead the conversation away from bicycles.

'Carving knife's blunt. Why women can't keep tools sharp always did beat me,' he mumbled, sawing away as though at a tree trunk.

'Marsdie's usually pretty good at keeping knives sharpened,' Susan said, determined that nothing should be said against Marsdie in her absence.

At last the meat and vegetables were served, some little time past the usual dinner hour, it was true, which perhaps accounted for the fact that everyone was more than usually hungry. Rather silently they began to eat.

'Oh!' Ruth exclaimed suddenly, choking a little.

'What's the matter?' Roger asked quickly.

'How tough the meat is! It's as stringy as leather.'

'So is mine! And the potatoes are as hard as stones,' Susan put in.

'My carrot and turnip are the same,' Dan chirruped.

'Now, you pipe down, young Dan, and just chew a bit harder,' Roger said rather shortly.

'Perhaps we ought to have kept to the instructions in the book,' Simon remarked thoughtfully, only to be frowned at by Roger. His words, however, had given Ruth a clue.

'How long did you cook the beef?' she asked.

'Oh, about an hour,' Roger answered carelessly.

'An hour? Only an hour?'

'It was boiling fast, of course,' Roger added by way of excuse.

'Oh, Roger, this kind of meat has to be cooked for hours very slowly, just *simmering*.'

'How was I to know? It was what the butcher sent, anyway. I had to do something with it.'

'But you should never let the butcher send you just what he thinks fit, should you, Ruth? That's where shopping comes in,' Susan informed Roger with a little self-righteous air.

'Don't preach, Susan! We've all got to learn by experience,' Simon snubbed his twin.

'Aye, that's right, Simon.' Sam Mitton grinned wickedly at Ruth and Susan. 'It's the same thing when you come to mend punctures. *Experience* is what counts.'

A strange silence descended upon Ruth and Susan for a minute or two. Susan even tried another mouthful of the unpalatable meat course.

'Anyway, there's a scrumptious pudding to follow,' Roger cheered them. 'Paradise pudding. You can smell how delicious it is.'

'I can smell it all right,' Ruth agreed, a little sinisterly.

'I'll go and get it out of the pan now while you're finishing off your first course,' Roger offered.

'While we're finishing off what we can eat of it, you mean,' Susan said cleverly.

'Oh, don't be so smart, Susan! Anyone can make mistakes,' Simon glared at her.

'Any road, it's a gradely pudding, you'll see,' Sam smiled round the table.

Just then a piercing yell came from the scullery where Roger was lifting the pudding from the pan. Ruth rushed from the table.

'What's the matter, Roger?'

'This pan is just red hot. I've scorched my hand.'

46

'Let me look,' Ruth said.

The rest of the Brydons and Sam came crowding round. Ruth peered at the pan and then cried in accusing tones, 'Why, you've let the pan boil dry. Look at that gas jet flaming away underneath. Lift the lid of the pan and you'll see there's not a spot of water in it.' Then, as Roger made to do what she said, Ruth seized his arm. 'No, take the fire tongs to it, if you don't want to burn yourself again.'

'Oh, my!' Roger groaned when he lifted the lid.

'Goodness, what a mess!' Simon exclaimed.

The basin had cracked in two and the pudding was sticking to the bottom of the red-hot pan.

'No wonder we could smell something like hot cake,' Susan declared.

Ruth, however, rose nobly to the occasion. 'Cheer up, Roger. It may not be absolutely uneatable,' she consoled him. 'Give me a large spoon. I think I can salvage enough for all of us. Hand me the pudding dishes one by one and I'll serve the pudding straight on to them. You're going to have an awful business getting this pan clean, though.'

Roger threw Ruth quite a grateful look. Once more the Brydons and Sam resumed their seats at the table. Politely Roger passed a bottle of orangeade to Susan.

'I hadn't any fruit to make a fruit sauce, so Dan thought this might do instead.'

'Ugh! No thanks,' Susan shuddered.

'Orangeade sauce, Ruth?'

'No thank you, Roger. I'll try the pudding without it first,' Ruth replied, equally politely.

Suddenly Dan choked on the spoonful he had put into his mouth.

'Oh, it's as salt as the sea,' he cried, regarding his portion with extreme distaste. Others of them screwed up their faces, too. Ruth began to turn the pudding over with her fork.

'What are all these pieces of skin?' she inquired.

'Perhaps that's the apple peeling. Maybe we should have peeled those apples after all, Dan,' Roger surmised.

Suddenly Susan gave a little horrified cry of pain. 'Heavens! What's this! I almost broke a tooth on it. It's like a brown stone. Thank goodness I didn't swallow it!'

'That'll probably be the nutmeg, Susan, that's all,' Simon said in a vain attempt to reassure her.

'Paradise pudding, indeed! Why, you've got half the Garden of Eden in it. Certainly the nuts and apple rinds are there,' Susan gibed.

'Of course, *you* would get the nutmeg, Susan,' Roger said savagely.

'Please may I put mine in the dustbin, Roger. I really can't eat it,' Dan asked meekly.

Coming from his own team, this was positively the last straw for Roger.

'You can jolly well go and do what you like with it. I'm through with cooking for such an ungrateful lot of folk,' he flared in a temper.

Dan got up from his place and carried his plate out into the garden. The others sat on in silence, wondering whether they would have the courage to follow Dan's lead. Suddenly, through the kitchen window, there came the sound of an appalling crash.

'Mercy me! What's that?' Ruth cried.

They all jumped from their chairs and ran to the

window. There was Dan lying in a heap, all mixed up with the bicycle and its dismantled tyres and an over-turned bucket of water.

'Dan! Dan! Are you hurt?' Ruth cried, rushing to help him to extricate himself.

'Not much. Only soaking wet!' Dan said ruefully. 'Why on earth did you have to leave that inner tube straggling like a snake all over the path? I caught my foot in it and brought the bike down on top of me and upset the bucket, too, as I fell. I'm just drenched.'

'Oh dear! I'm so sorry, Dan, but why didn't you look where you were going?' Ruth replied.

'Eeh, everything seems in a proper mess, doesn't it?' Sam said unhappily. 'Nowt seems to be going right. Things seem 'witched.'

'You're right, Sam,' Ruth concurred heartily. 'Things are just 'witched. I wish Marsdie was home again.'

From the heartfelt way in which the others applauded this remark it was evidently their sentiment also.

CHAPTER FOUR

Mrs Hallam has a tea-party

IT was well into the middle of the afternoon before the boys had finished the rather greasy washing-up and Roger had more or less successfully scoured the bottom of the burnt pan. Dan and Sam disappeared on some mysterious errand of their own which took them in the direction of Milchester, while Roger and Simon set about their belated task of tidying up and weeding the vegetable garden ready for the St Jonathan's Garden Party next day.

Roger had secretly hoped that Ruth might relent and appear at the little green door in the wall to announce that tea was ready, but, as the afternoon wore on and the position of the sun indicated that it was tea-time, no clatter of cups came from the kitchen of One Elm Cottage. Roger put down his hoe rather dismally.

'I've got a job of work to do in the house, Simon. I'll put the kettle on the gas ring, but when you've finished raking that path, come and give me a hand, will you?'

Simon nodded and Roger betook himself to the house. On the way he stopped for a moment to unpeg a white flannel shirt from the clothes line. Ten minutes later when Simon followed him into the cottage, he found Roger just starting work on the ironing board.

'What are you doing?' he exclaimed in surprise.

'Just a spot of ironing,' Roger replied airily, as though

this were quite a customary occupation for him. 'Where are the girls? I haven't seen them for a long time.'

'They went off towards Beechacres not long after dinner, and they called out that very likely they wouldn't be back for tea.'

'Oh, they did, did they?' Roger said darkly. 'Were they on their bicycles? Did Ruth get that puncture mended?'

Simon shook his head. 'I imagine they *thought* they'd mended it, for they got the tyre on again and trundled the bicycles into the wash-house; but that tyre's gone as flat as a pancake again.'

'Well, that's their pigeon,' Roger commented rather vindictively. 'You know, I'd have given Ruth a hand with that puncture if she hadn't been so snooty about my shirt.'

'Your shirt?' Simon appeared mystified.

'Yes. I wanted it for the Garden Party tomorrow. It's my only white flannel shirt, and I suddenly found this morning that I'd forgotten to put it out to wash after that last cricket match at school. I mentioned it to Ruth, casually, you know, saying I'd be needing it tomorrow, and she said, "Go ahead. You know where the wash-tub is" – just like that.'

Simon nodded with sympathy. 'You know, I'm begining to think this business of changing jobs isn't so very hot after all.'

Dan and Sam appeared in the kitchen just in time to catch Simon's words.

'I'm jolly sure it isn't,' Dan agreed. 'What are you going to do with that frying-pan, Simon?'

'Getting ready to cook the kippers for tea.'

'Oh, I *am* glad. We're jolly hungry after that dreadful dinner, aren't we, Sam?'

'Just about clemmed,' Sam put it bluntly.

'You ungrateful little beasts!' Roger snorted.

'It was a pity your mother was out, Sam, and she'd taken the door-key with her,' Dan remarked regretfully.

'Oh, so you've been to see,' Roger sniffed.

'Will you be long on that table, Roger? I want to set it for tea,' Simon called from the scullery where he was busy over the frying-pan.

'Only a minute or two. I must iron this shirt and I've just got the iron nice and hot. It won't take long. It'll be done by the time you've finished the kippers.'

'Very well,' Simon agreed.

Roger with great enthusiasm started ironing at a tremendous pace. ' "Dashing away with the smoothing iron",' he sang with great spirit, but gradually both tune and words began to slow down and come in jerks, till finally he broke off altogether. For the fourth time he lifted the shirt from the table and shook it vigorously.

'Bother this shirt!' he exclaimed, banging the iron down. 'As fast as I iron the back, the front wrinkles up again, and when I turn to the front, the back just gets into a mass of creases. Why shirts are made like this, I can't imagine.'

Once more he thumped away with the iron, but this time he did not break into song. Simon put his head round the scullery door.

'I say, Roger, is a kipper done when it turns black?'

'I should jolly well think it is. Done *for*!' Roger pronounced.

'Oh!' was all Simon said with a very crestfallen air.

'Here! Let me look,' Roger said, putting down the iron and rushing into the scullery to inspect the contents of the frying-pan. 'Why, that's nothing but a cinder, Simon Brydon. You'll have to eat that yourself.'

'Oh, all right,' Simon snapped, with an unusual show of temper for his usual quiet nature.

'Give me the frying-pan,' Roger said, seizing the handle in his hand and putting more cooking fat into the pan. 'You didn't put enough dripping in. I'll cook my own kipper, and then I know it will be all right.'

'I didn't know you were so wonderful at cooking as all that,' Dan said cheekily, the memory of Roger's recent failure with the dinner being still very fresh.

'That's enough. No cheek from you, young Dan,' Roger rebuked him sternly.

'I can smell summut burning, Roger,' Sam said, sniffing the air like a terrier puppy.

'Oh, that'll be Sam's kipper. He's made a burnt offering of it,' Roger jeered a little unkindly.

'You know, I think the girls might have taken pity on us and stopped at home and made the tea,' Dan grumbled. 'There'll be the washing-up to do again afterwards, and it will be jolly greasy, too, after those kippers.'

'Oh, don't be so sorry for yourself, Dan,' Roger exclaimed in exasperation. 'Anyone would think you were the worst sufferer. I wonder where the girls have gone, all the same.'

'Perhaps to see Miss Miggs,' Simon hazarded a guess.

'I wish we'd thought of going to see Miss Miggs, Sam,' Dan remarked with very real regret.

'Aye, lad, it's any port in a storm, as you might say,' Sam agreed in heartfelt tones.

'Oh, Miss Miggs is rather a good sort' – Dan put in a good word in her favour. 'Look how she fished me out of Milchester Tarn last Christmas when the ice broke.'

'Yes, she's one of the best when you get to know her,' Roger seconded. 'Now, look at that.' He held the frying-pan towards them. 'That's how a kipper should be done – a delicate brown on both sides,' he pointed out proudly.

'Then what is it I can smell, Roger? It's getting stronger. It's a – a kind of *scorching* smell.' Sam sniffed again.

Roger dropped the frying-pan on the stove as though he had been stung by a wasp.

'Golly! My shirt! I've left it on the kitchen table with the iron on it!'

Roger dashed back into the kitchen with the others at his heels. Too late, he snatched the iron from his smoking shirt and switched off the electric current.

'Is it burnt?' Simon asked needlessly.

Too horrified for words, Roger held up his shirt. A blackened patch the shape and size of the iron appeared in the front of it.

'Mercy me!' was all he could find to say. 'What a mess!'

'What'll you do for the Garden Party now, Roger?' Dan asked, really concerned for his brother.

'Eh, Roger, I'm proper sorry about it,' Sam sympathized.

'What the dickens am I to wear tomorrow? That's my only cricket shirt.' Roger found words at last.

'And you can't buy them in Milchester, either. I remember Marsdie saying she had to hunt the shops in Preston to get that one,' Simon informed him.

'It's a proper-to-do,' Sam said solemnly.

'Well, you can't do anything about it now, Roger, so we may as well have tea,' Dan remarked rather tactlessly in a matter-of-fact tone.

'Tea! I don't feel like any tea,' Roger groaned.

'I do, after that horrible dinner,' Dan reminded him.

'You're nothing but a heartless little brute, Dan. Get your own teas,' he flung at them, then dashed out of the kitchen, slamming the door behind him. For a moment the others stared at the closed door, then Dan shrugged his shoulders.

'I'm not awfully keen on kippers anyway, are you, Sam? Come along. Let's go and see Mrs Hallam. Friday's the day she always bakes.'

Dan winked solemnly at Sam, who, with ready understanding, followed him out of One Elm Cottage and through the little green door into the Beechacres garden.

*   *   *

Over in the kitchen at Beechacres Mrs Hallam already had two unexpected guests. Ruth and Susan had spent what was left of the afternoon with Sister Jones, helping to arrange the Handwork display, so as to save Miss Marsden time and trouble on her return home. They had hoped that she would be back by tea-time and that her presence at the tea-table would bring back the usual happy atmosphere at One Elm Cottage. Ruth was really troubled at being out of friends with Roger. It was indeed a rare thing for them to quarrel, and both of them were rather sick and sore about it, but, as Simon said, neither of them would climb down. So, when tea-time came round,

Ruth and Susan found themselves, almost by chance, in Mrs Hallam's shining kitchen. Soon they were seated at the table with the yellow-and-white checked cloth, and Mrs Hallam poured out tea from the brown earthenware tea-pot which had been her mother's, and which, she declared, with reason, made better tea than any other she knew.

'These little cakes are awfully good, Mrs Hallam. Will you give me the recipe sometime?' Ruth asked. She collected recipes from all her friends and was compiling a cookery book of her own.

'Eh, love, I made them out of my own head. I don't know if I can remember what I put in 'em,' Mrs Hallam confessed.

'Then it's a loss to the world, Mrs Hallam,' Susan sighed.

Mrs Hallam was so touched by this tribute to her baking that she passed the cake dish again to Susan.

'Have another, Susan, love.'

'Oh, thanks, I was hoping you'd ask me,' Susan naïvely confessed.

'It was awfully nice of you to ask us to stay to tea today,' Ruth said gratefully.

'Well, seeing it was close on tea-time when you dropped in, I thought there was no sense in having it by miself. I likes a bit of company, you know. My mother used to say – and she was a wise woman – "Even bread tastes better if you eat it wi' friends".'

Susan looked through the window and saw Dan and Sam just crossing the lawn towards the kitchen door.

'It's a good thing you like company, Mrs Hallam, for it looks as if you're going to have two more visitors. I can see Dan and Sam Mitton coming across the garden.'

'If that's not the limit!' Ruth exclaimed, rather vexed.

'Eh, ne'er mind, Ruth. They're welcome,' Mrs Hallam said comfortably. 'I was wondering where the lads were and what they were doing, seeing Miss Marsden's at Preston,' she added with a native insight that she must have inherited from her wise mother. Ruth and Susan exchanged glances, but said nothing. Just then there came a tap at the door and in answer to Mrs Hallam's 'Come in', the two chums peered round the door.

'Good afternoon, Mrs Hallam. Sam and I thought we'd drop in to visit you, seeing we haven't seen you for – for a whole day,' Dan began in his most polite society manner. His face fell, however, when he opened the door a little wider and discovered Ruth and Susan already in possession. 'Oh, hullo, girls!' he exclaimed in not very enthusiastic tones. 'We didn't know you were here.'

'No, I guessed as much,' Ruth replied with some sarcasm.

Mrs Hallam, however, scenting a difference, beckoned the boys farther into the room.

'Come in, Dan. Come in, Sam, love. Just wipe your feet on the mat and pull in your chairs to the table.'

'It's proper nice of you to make us so welcome, Mrs Hallam. My mother's out, or we might have gone there,' Sam Mitton said with his usual honest bluntness. Dan trod heavily upon his toe.

'What's up, Dan?' Sam asked. 'Have I dropped a brick or summut? I only said my mother was out.'

Before Sam could expostulate further, however, Mrs Hallam had them seated at the table and the tea poured out. Hardly had she done this, however, than there was another tap at the door. The door was opened and round it peeped Miss Marsden.

'Marsdie!' everyone cried with delight.

'Good gracious, Mrs Hallam, you are having an At Home day!' she laughed. 'I just called to deliver the crockery for tomorrow and what do I find? All my family here – at least, nearly all.'

'Now, just come in, Miss Marsden, do. The crockery can wait till you've had a cup of tea. I'll give you a hand with it afterwards. If I know anything, you'll be just about dying for that cup of tea,' Mrs Hallam smiled.

'Mrs Hallam, my tongue is indeed cleaving to the roof of my mouth,' Marsdie chuckled. 'You're an angel. Lead me to the tea-pot.'

'You're much later than we expected, Marsdie,' Ruth said.

'Yes. We had a horrid puncture this side of Preston on the return journey, and had to change the wheel. After that, I decided I'd better get the puncture mended right away at a garage, in case the car was needed tomorrow, so we had another wait while it was done.'

'We went on with setting out the Handwork display, along with Sister Jones, this afternoon,' Susan told her.

'Good girls, thanks so much. Oh, I've brought a lot of flags and bunting back with me, too. The crockery man put us wise as to where we could hire it very cheaply. Actually, the people lent it us for nothing when they heard that the Garden Party was for the little patients at St Jonathan's. I shall want Roger and Simon to help me to fix it up after tea. By the way, where is Roger?'

'Roger said he wasn't keen about having any tea,' Dan explained.

'What was wrong with the *tea* at One Elm Cottage?' Susan inquired pertly.

'Not keen about tea? He wasn't ill, was he?' Miss Marsden looked very puzzled.

Dan realized that he had said either too much or too little, but Sam, as usual, blurted out the blunt truth.

'No. It was after a bit of bother over his shirt, you see,' he explained. Sam's explanation, however, only served to befog things more than ever.

'His shirt?' Marsdie asked, absolutely mystified.

'We may as well tell them all about it now, seeing you've put your foot in it so far, Sam,' Dan said resignedly. 'Roger was ironing his cricket shirt for tomorrow, and while he was frying a kipper he left the iron on his shirt and it burnt a piece clean out.'

'Eeh, the poor lamb! Did you ever?' Mrs Hallam threw up her hands in consternation.

'And after that he didn't feel like any tea, you see,' Sam supplied the tail ending miserably.

'But why was Roger ironing his shirt and cooking kippers at the same time?' Marsdie was curious to know.

Ruth and Susan looked guiltily at each other.

'Now, what's gone wrong over at One Elm Cottage today?' Mrs Hallam asked, setting down the tea-pot.

'It was a silly sort of game,' Ruth began, rather unhappily. 'At least, it didn't really start as a game,' she admitted. 'Roger and I got mad at each other all about mending my bicycle and the different jobs we had to do –

stupid things really – and then we all started taking sides and in the end we all said we'd do each other's jobs and show how much better we could do them.'

'Only it didn't quite work out that way,' Susan confessed a little shamefacedly.

'You're right, Susan, it didn't. Oh, that dinner!' Dan groaned in a heartfelt way.

'It all looks so very silly now,' Ruth said.

'Aye, "when tempers pop up, common sense flies out of the window", as my mother used to say . . .' Mrs Hallam began.

' "And she was a wise woman",' Dan quoted almost by force of habit. 'Oh, I mean it, Mrs Hallam,' he hastened to add, lest his sincerity should be misunderstood.

'She was that! Well, now, Dan, just you nip across to One Elm Cottage and tell those two poor lads there's a cup of tea waiting for 'em in my kitchen.'

Without needing any second bidding Dan was off, and in two or three minutes returned with a rather crestfallen Roger, accompanied by Simon. Very little was said by either side, except to greet Marsdie, until Roger had reached his second cup of tea.

'Come along, Roger, pass up your cup again. I can see it's empty,' Mrs Hallam invited him.

'Thanks a lot, Mrs Hallam. This tea is very refreshing. It kind of heartens one up, you know.'

'Aye, it's not been very smooth going over at One Elm Cottage, I understand.' Mrs Hallam nodded her head wisely.

Miss Marsden looked from Roger to Ruth in a rather quizzical manner.

'No, it's not been smooth,' Roger admitted with a

twinkle in his eye. 'But it's been quite – er – *instructive*, hasn't it, Ruth?'

'You're right, Roger. Oh, that puncture!'

'Oh, my shirt!'

Both suddenly burst out laughing, and that spontaneous laughter did more to clear the air than anything else. All round the table faces relaxed.

'We've been a pair of idiots, Roger,' Ruth said frankly.

'You're right, Ruth. We have, and I'm sorry. I can't think how it started, really.'

'Neither can I. Look here, I'll patch your shirt for you this evening,' Ruth offered handsomely.

'And I'll patch your puncture, and then we'll be quits,' Roger grinned, not to be outdone in generosity.

'Now, that's something like!' Mrs Hallam nodded in approval. 'I began to wonder what was ailing you both. As my mother used to say, and she was a wise woman, "Solder a broken pipe and it's often stronger. Make up a quarrel and your friendship's sweeter".'

Everyone smiled approval of this sentiment.

'It's just been a kind of game of "Family Coach", and now you're all back in your right places again,' Marsdie said.

'What's "Family Coach", Marsdie?' Dan asked.

'Oh, it's just a game where everyone is a part of the Family Coach, the wheels, the reins, the box-seat – anything you like. Someone makes up a story about the Family Coach and whenever your particular bit is mentioned, you dash to change places. But I think the truth is that no Family Coach can run smoothly unless everyone is playing his or her proper part.'

'Well, there's more to mending punctures than I thought,' Ruth acknowledged.

'And there's certainly a lot more to making a dinner,' Roger admitted gallantly.

'And now, *mes enfants*, I've got an awful lot of jobs for the Brydon Family Coach. There are all those yards and yards of bunting and flags to string up, and the men with the marquee should be here shortly.' Marsdie set down her cup.

'Come along, Ruth. Let's work together. We'd better beat it to get hold of the tools before Sister Jones does. Marsdie's got that chivvying look in her eye.' Roger grinned with his usual impudence.

CHAPTER FIVE

St Jonathan's Garden Party

SATURDAY proved to be one of the loveliest days in all that lovely July. Only the fleeciest, most lamb-like clouds sailed in the blue heaven, and a gentle breath of a breeze kept the air stirring enough to prevent the sunshine from being too oppressively hot. It was an ideal day for St Jonathan's Garden Party. As it was, it proved just warm enough to promote a lively sale of iced drinks and steaming cups of tea, dispensed by smiling Mrs Hallam and her assistants. If anything, they were far hotter than most of the contestants in the sports, but they maintained a cheerful good nature. On the sports ground there were races to suit everyone, and everyone, indeed, took part. Under the able organization of Mr Cameron, Professor Brydon, Roger, and Sister Jones, the sports took place while the Milchester Prize Band played popular music under a shady clump of trees. Practically all the village of Milchester had turned out for this great occasion and had brought all their friends and relations from outlying places, too, to support the effort made by the little patients at St Jonathan's, helped by Miss Marsden and the Brydon family.

Dr Brydon and Miss Marsden strolled happily among the crowd, greeting friends and acquaintances everywhere.

'I do think it's kind of the Milchester Prize Band to come and play for our garden party. They offered of their own accord, you know,' Dr Brydon said.

Marsdie chuckled. 'Yes, Sam Mitton saw to that. "Grandfaither" Mitton still plays a handsome trombone, I hear. I've an idea that Sam applied a little friendly coercion to "Grandfaither".'

'Good for Sam! He always persuades the Milchester people to help St Jonathan's Hospital here – not that they need much persuading: they're too kind.'

'They always do rally round,' Marsdie agreed.

'The band seems to be coming to the end of its programme,' Dr Brydon remarked, as the climax seemed to be arriving of 'D'ye Ken John Peel?' played in masterly style with a special View Halloa by the cornet-player.

'I think we're almost at the end of the races, too,' Miss Marsden said with a twinkle in her eye. 'But, look: Mr Cameron's going to say something to the crowd. Let's listen.'

Mr Cameron was standing on the terrace with his megaphone to his mouth.

'That concludes the programme of our races, ladies and gentlemen, with the exception of one race,' he announced. 'For this last race Miss Marsden has made a suggestion to me. She thinks it would be a good idea to have a special race for the Milchester Prize Band.'

There was much applause for this announcement, which changed into hearty laughter when Mr Cameron went on, 'We shall expect them all to play on their instruments as they run, of course. Will all the bandsmen line up at the tape with their instruments, please?'

There was a humorous stampede on the part of the

bandsmen, and much friendly jostling for an inside position on the tape.

'Eh, Mister Cameron, it's not fair that us owd 'uns should be lined up alongside all these young chaps,' one elderly bandsman objected.

Mr Cameron saw the force of this at once. 'That's right enough, Mr Forshaw. Now, will everyone who is over fifty please take a long stride for each additional year of his age.'

The older bandsmen were quick to take advantage of this concession. Sam's grandfather began to chuckle as he strode forward, carrying his trombone at the ready.

'Eh, look at Grandfaither Mitton. He's nigh at t'finishing post afore the race has started,' one of the young bandsmen objected, but his objection was drowned in roars of laughter from the other bandsmen.

'Well, he's seventy-five, isn't he?' Sam Mitton piped up indignantly, vociferous on his grandfather's behalf. 'He deserves a start, doesn't he?'

'Grandfaither' Mitton solemnly closed one eye at Sam. Holding his trombone between his knees, he licked the palms of his hands and rubbed them together, then fixed his eye with a 'Do or Die' expression on the finishing post.

Mr Cameron gave the competitors their directions. 'Now, when I blow the whistle, will you all run forward, playing your instruments. If anyone stops playing, he will be disqualified immediately.'

The race began with a blare of horrid sounds as every bandsman seemed to have selected a different tune to play. To this din were added the cheers and laughter of the spectators. Miss Marsden put her fingers in her ears, and became helpless with laughter as she watched the drummer struggling along under the awkward burden of his drum, which would get in the way of his knees when he tried to run. Sam Mitton ran alongside his grandfather, with Dan Brydon at the other side, both of them shrieking at the top of their voices as they exhorted him to greater efforts.

'Go on, Grandfaither, go on! Don't stop blowing at your trombone.'

The cornet player laughed so much at the desperate working of the slide on Grandfaither Mitton's trombone, that he failed to produce a tune from his cornet and was instantly disqualified by Mr Cameron. Grandfaither Mitton struggled valiantly on amid the roars of the crowd.

'Oh, well done, Grandfaither Mitton! He's leading and he's still playing a very handsome trombone,' Marsdie applauded, clapping her hands.

'Go on, Grandfaither Mitton! Go on! You're winning,' the crowd shrieked. 'Well done, Grandfaither Mitton.'

The first to reach the finishing tape, Grandfaither Mitton continued to tootle triumphantly a few bars of 'Hearts of Oak' ending with 'We'll Fight and We'll Conquer Again and Again' in a most victorious fashion.

'Splendid, Grandfaither Mitton, splendid!' Mr Cameron applauded.

'Aye, there's still plenty of life in the owd mon yet.' Grandfaither Mitton winked one eye.

'I think we might as well follow up the last race right away with the distribution of prizes, seeing that we've got the crowd already assembled,' Mr Cameron decided. 'Dr Brydon, if you're ready now, I'll be pleased if you'll present the prizes for the sports.'

'Willingly,' Dr Brydon consented. 'Where shall we stand?'

'On the terrace here, I think. Everyone can see us and hear us quite easily then.' Mr Cameron raised his megaphone to his lips. 'Gather round, everybody, please. The children had better come to the front and sit down, then they'll see all that's going on.'

There was a minute or two of confusion while the good-natured crowd sorted itself out and gave the children positions at the front, then the cheerful murmuring died away while they waited to hear what Mr Cameron had to say.

'I'm not going to make a speech, because I'm not a bit clever at making speeches,' he announced. 'But right now I have a pleasant little duty to perform. I'm going to ask Dr Brydon to present the prizes for the sports, with a few *running* comments from me.' Mr Cameron chuckled at his own joke. 'First, I think the little patients at St Jonathan's are to be congratulated on the way they have overcome all their difficulties and have taken part in every event open to them. I'm sure you'll all be pleased to know that Dr Brydon thinks that with time and care they'll all be running about like healthy normal children again. I wish I could give these plucky little people a first prize each.'

There was a storm of hand-clapping and cheering to greet this remark. When it died away, Mr Cameron continued, 'Now for the prizes, if Dr Brydon will kindly step forward.' He referred to a list of names and events in his hand. 'The Egg and Spoon race: this was won by Clara Cox, who carried her egg very steadily all the way. Well done, Clara! Katy Dollan was nearly first, but she let her egg roll off just before the finishing-post. Honourable mention, Katy, and for all those anxious spectators, who have been wondering about the eggs, may I state they were only the pot ones that encourage the hens to produce the real article.'

Clara Cox came shyly forward and received from Dr Brydon a very pretty china egg cup in the shape of a chicken. It had once been Susan's, but she had very generously given it as a prize for this particular race. Clara bore it away in high glee to show to Sister Jones, and Mr Cameron passed on to the next announcement on his list.

'The Apple and Lemonade race: in this race, you may remember, everyone had to eat an apple and drink a cup of lemonade in record time. This was easily won outright by Charlie Carter, despite the awful warnings uttered by Sister Jones.'

Charlie came forward, his freckled face screwed up into a grin at Sister Jones.

'I have much pleasure in handing you the first prize, Charlie.' Dr Drydon smiled at her oldest and well loved patient. 'It's a stick of rock, together with a digestive tablet of Gregory's Mixture from Sister Jones.'

The little patients of St Jonathan's hooted with laughter, for there was a constant good-natured state of feud existing between Charlie Carter and Sister Jones.

'Don't you dare to tell me you've got the tummy-ache tonight, Charlie Carter,' Sister Jones pretended to warn him fiercely.

'And now for the prize for the Buried Treasure Hunt,' Mr Cameron announced. 'We might have called it "Hunt the Slipper" for it was really Sister Jones's slipper that we hid.'

'Indeed, to goodness!' Sister Jones exclaimed at this amazing piece of news.

'I regret to say it was found by Dog Jonathan,' Mr Cameron went on, unable to suppress a little giggle. 'He was last seen rushing round in circles with it in his mouth, and he refused to give it up. He must have hidden it again where no one can find it, so I declare the Treasure Hunt still open.'

Sister Jones's face was a study in surprise and mock indignation.

'But, as a consolation prize for all the disappointed hunters, every patient in St Jonathan's is to have a large ice-cream cornet as a present from me. Mrs Hallam will dispense them in the marquee after the prize-giving is over,' Mr Cameron told them with a happy smile.

This announcement brought the greatest applause yet, and shrill cheers from all the boys and girls.

'And I'll offer a reward of another stick of rock to the finder,' Sister Jones called out. 'My good slipper, look you,' she added a trifle regretfully.

'If it never turns up I'll make some leather moccasins for you, Sister Jones,' Miss Marsden promised in a whisper.

'Maybe I should encourage Dog Jonathan to run away with my gloves too,' Sister Jones replied in another impish whisper.

'The Good-night Race, in which everyone had to run with a lighted candle and blow it out at the finishing post was a neck and neck affair between Sister Jones and Miss Marsden. Miss Marsden might have won, but she forgot to blow out her candle.'

The Brydons could not refrain from laughing – it was so like Marsdie! She, however, denied it indignantly.

'Oh, no, I didn't! I'd no breath left.'

'Well done, Sister Jones!' Dr Brydon shook hands with her assistant and handed her the well-won prize. 'I know this electric torch will be more use to you than a candle when you go round to see every one of these little people safely tucked up for the night.'

Sister Jones was tremendously pleased. 'This will help me to look round a corner to see what mischief Charlie Carter is up to,' she laughed.

'I think everyone enjoyed our most novel *washing-up* race,' Mr Cameron said. 'You remember, six mugs, plates, and spoons had to be washed up in record time. This was won by – guess who? – Dan Brydon, though his methods, I might mention, would *not* have won him a prize in a college of Domestic Science, and I did hear someone whisper that it was a jolly good thing that the dishes were all enamel ones.'

Amid laughter and ironic cheers from the rest of the Brydon family, Dr Brydon said, 'Dan, I have great pleasure in conferring upon you the Order of the Dish Clout,' and presented her son with an outsize in dish cloths.

Dan was distinctly taken aback with the form his prize took.

'Well, I never guessed I'd win a *dish cloth*. Had you anything to do with this, Ruth?' Ruth could only giggle in reply, but Marsdie exclaimed, 'Up the dish washers, Dan! There's been a lot of good work wasted in you.'

The very last prize to be presented was the one for the special race run by the Milchester Prize Band. This was two ounces of tobacco, specially presented for the race by Mr Cameron, and won, of course, by Mr Sam Mitton, senior, otherwise known to all Milchester as 'Grandfaither Mitton'. This little ceremony of presenting the prize was great fun, as the Milchester Prize Band escorted him to receive it, all playing 'See the Conquering Hero Comes'.

'Splendid, Grandfaither Mitton, splendid!' Dr Brydon congratulated him. 'I hope you enjoy your smoke to-night.'

'To be sure, I will, ma'am. Thank'ee. I reckon I deserved it, even if I did have a start o' twenty-five yards o'er t'others, and Bob Walker said he held back wi' t'drum to let me win. But I'd like to remind 'em I had a start o' twenty-five *years* and a good bit more o'er t'most of 'em.'

He retired amid loud applause to stuff his pipe with part of his well-earned prize.

'And that, friends, concludes our prize list,' Mr Cameron announced. 'But I am going to ask you to give a special cheer for Miss Marsden, who had the first idea for this garden party and sports day, and who was really responsible for its organization.'

All Milchester joined in the hearty cheer which the St Jonathan's patients and the Brydons gave, for Miss Marsden was most popular with old and young alike.

'No, no!' she protested. 'Oh, really, really, everyone helped, and it's all been tremendous fun.' But the cheering only became louder.

'And now I must announce the happy result of our united effort,' Mr Cameron continued, as soon as he was able to make himself heard again. 'Though we are not yet quite sure of the exact amount of money we have raised, through the helpful generosity of our Milchester friends in coming here today, we know that we have made sufficient funds to take our little patients for a day's outing by motor coach. You little people of St Jonathan's have the satisfaction of knowing you've *earned* the money yourselves, by your own hard efforts, and that's a very great thing. And now, I'd like everyone to be my guest for tea in the marquee. And while you're having it, the Milchester Prize Band has offered to play some selections. Thank you all very much.'

With that, Mr Cameron and Dr Brydon stepped down from the terrace amid much hand-clapping. There followed a rush to the marquee where Mrs Hallam, Ruth, and several helpers from the village were already installed behind the tea-urns and cups. As they began dispensing the tea, the Milchester Prize Band struck up a lively selection from the Gilbert and Sullivan operas.

CHAPTER SIX

Plan for a picnic

Two or three weeks later the Brydon family, Miss Marsden, Mr Cameron, and Sister Jones were all assembled in Mr Cameron's library at Beechacres. They had met together to discuss how the money should be spent which had been raised by the garden party, and what arrangements should be made for the picnic outing.

'Is everybody here?' Roger asked rather impatiently. 'Can we start discussing things?' He was anxious to get the meeting started so that it would not be too late for him when it had finished to put in some cricket practice with the Milchester Cricket Club which he had recently joined.

'We can't start for a minute or two, Roger. Mrs Hallam isn't here yet,' Ruth pointed out.

'Oh, we can't start without Mrs Hallam,' Miss Marsden declared. 'She's got more common sense than the rest of us put together.'

'I quite agree, Miss Marsden,' Mr Cameron seconded with a twinkle in his eye. 'Especially when we reckon the wisdom of her wise mother as well. Oh, yes, we'll need Mrs Hallam.'

'Where is she, then?' Roger wanted to know. 'Did anyone remember to tell her about this meeting?'

'Yes, I did,' Susan said.

'Just cut along to the kitchen, then, Dan, and tell Mrs Hallam we're all waiting for her.'

Just then the door opened and the stout comfortable figure of Mrs Hallam was framed in the doorway.

'No need, Roger, love. Here I am, clap on the dot of time.'

'Five minutes since the dot was clapped, Mrs Hallam,' Roger corrected her.

Mrs Hallam cast a glance at the grandfather clock in the corner. 'Eeh, so it is! Well, would you believe? Come to think, though, I did stop to lay out the cups and saucers on a tray and to put the kettle on. My mother used to say — and she was a wise woman — "Talking oils the tongue but it makes the throat proper dry".'

'Blessings on your wise mother, Mrs Hallam,' Miss Marsden chuckled with approval. 'It's a thirsty afternoon.'

'I think you should take the chair at this meeting, Mr Cameron,' Roger urged, anxious to get on with the business.

Mr Cameron, however, was not to be so easily persuaded.

'Good gracious, Roger, you make me feel quite nervous, it sounds so very important.' He looked round for a substitute. 'What about you, Dr Brydon?'

Dr Brydon, however, shook her head vigorously. 'No, no, Mr Cameron. This is my afternoon off, if you please –'

'Then Miss Marsden, perhaps? Now, Marsdie –'

'Goodness me, no! I'd be constantly losing track of the proceedings. You know how forgetful I am.'

'Now, Marsdie, you know you're just using that as an excuse *not* to take the chair,' Ruth accused her.

'What's the good of having a bad memory if you can't use it for an excuse sometimes?' Marsdie giggled. 'No, I'm going to pass the buck to Sister Jones. I think she'd fill the chair well.'

'Oh, no, I've never taken the chair at a meeting in my life,' Sister Jones declined hastily.

'Oh, it's quite simple, Sister Jones. You just call on people to give their ideas and make a note of what they say –' Roger began, but he was interrupted by Mr Cameron.

'I think the duty had better devolve on Roger this time, seeing that he seems to know so much about it. It'll be good practice for you for when you have to make speeches at college next term, Roger. I vote you into the chair.'

'Well, if I must, I must,' Roger agreed reluctantly. He took the chair at the head of the library table, cleared his throat, drew his brows together importantly, and began, 'Ahem! Ladies and Gentlemen.'

Susan simply had to laugh.

'Stop giggling, Susan,' Roger said sternly.

'Sorry!' Susan apologized with mock contrition. 'Everybody is looking as serious as an owl. If you could only see yourselves –'

'We'll bring mirrors to the meeting next time,' Roger rebuked her with heavy sarcasm. 'Now, let's get down to business. First of all, it's proper champion, as Sam Mitton says, that we've raised enough money by the garden party to take all the patients at St Jonathan's for a day's holiday by coach.'

Everyone applauded this remark, particularly Sister Jones.

'Indeed, it is, Roger. Most of the children have not been far outside the gates of Beechacres since they came here. It will be a delightful treat.'

'Good, Sister Jones. Now, first of all, which day shall we fix for the outing?' Roger went on in business-like fashion.

'Not a Saturday, Roger. Most places are too busy and crowded on Saturdays,' his mother said.

'I think Thursday would be a suitable, quiet day,' Miss Marsden suggested.

Instantly everyone agreed with this. 'Yes, Thursday. Let's choose Thursday.'

'We'd better have the outing soon, too, because once September comes in, we're getting ready for school again and it's soon dark at nights,' Simon put in.

'Good point, Simon,' Mr Cameron approved. 'Why not have the outing a week next Thursday? I think it could easily be arranged with the coach people.'

It was agreed that a week on Thursday would be a very convenient and suitable date, and Roger duly noted this very solemnly on his writing pad.

'Then the next point to be decided is – where shall we go?' Roger told the meeting.

'The top of Pendle Hill,' Susan suggested at once. She had always wanted to picnic on the top of Pendle Hill.

'Do we invite the Lancashire Witches, too?' Simon teased her.

Pendle Hill was the place once reputed to be the haunt of the Lancashire Witches, where they held their nightly revels. Dr Brydon, however, had other reasons why she thought Pendle would be unsuitable.

'It's too stiff a climb for most of the little patients of St Jonathan's, Susan.'

Susan saw this at once. 'Oh, yes, that's right, Mother.'

'What about Sam Mitton's aunt's farm at Stainfold?' Mr Cameron proposed. 'We all had a good time when we stayed there.'

Before anyone could reply to this suggestion, Mrs Hallam spoke up. 'If you'll pardon my making so bold, Mr Cameron, there's a farm across the road here in Milchester. Most of the St Jonathan's children play about there any time they fancy. A farm wouldn't be any change, like, for them. What they want is a right change, something different from Milchester, wi' all its fields around it.'

'I say, you've got something there, Mrs Hallam,' Roger nodded.

'Well, my mother always did say, "If you want to open your eyes wide, look at something out of the ordinary".'

'Mrs Hallam means the sea.' Dan interpreted her wisdom to suit his own wishes. 'There's no sea in Milchester. Oh, do let's go to the seaside. We'd have lots more fun there than anywhere.'

'Dan's right, you know,' Mr Cameron laughed. 'I've a sneaking hankering after the sea myself. What do you think of the idea, Dr Brydon?'

Dr Brydon hesitated a little. 'It's a very good idea, but I'm afraid the beaches at Blackpool or Southport will be rather crowded at this time of the year.'

'Couldn't we find a quiet seaside place, Mother?' Simon asked.

'Yes, somewhere far from the *maddening* crowd, as the poet says,' Dan added, as usual getting very mixed when he tried to use long words. Everyone chuckled. Dan's mistakes were proverbial.

'Unfortunately the poet didn't say how we were to feed the multitude of St Jonathan's when we'd left the "maddening" crowd behind, Dan,' Dr Brydon smiled. 'A deserted beach will hardly provide us with a hot dinner.'

'And we really ought to have some place like a schoolroom where the children can play if the weather turns showery. Imagine picnicking amid acres of sand in the midst of a sudden drenching thunderstorm.' Miss Marsden added her sensible contribution to the discussion.

'Marsdie's quite right. We must make some provision for shelter,' Dr Brydon said. 'Really, too, the children should have some place where they can have a quiet rest for half an hour after dinner, if the outing is to do them any good.'

'Indeed, yes, Dr Brydon,' Sister Jones chimed in. 'If Clara Cox doesn't get her after-dinner nap she's as cross as a wasp. Now, I've got an idea, if you would listen to me for one moment, please.'

'Go ahead, Sister Jones.' Roger gave his informal permission from the chair.

'I have a sister – the clever one of my family, she is: university and all that, you know,' Sister Jones told them, swelling with pride in her sister. 'A teacher she is, in a nice boarding-school near the sea front at West Kirby.'

'Where's West Kirby?' Simon asked.

'On the Wirral peninsula, just across the river Mersey from Liverpool, Simon, and West Kirby's near the point of the peninsula where the Mersey and the Dee meet. You can look across the Dee to the Welsh mountains,' Mr Cameron explained. He got a map out from a cupboard and showed them all the correct place on it.

'Go on, please, Sister Jones. Tell us some more about it,' Dr Brydon asked.

'The beach there is very good sand, and between West Kirby and Hoylake, near the golf links, it is quiet enough.'

'Yes, yes,' Mr Cameron said with interest.

'Then there is the school. Quite near to the beach it is,' Sister Jones declared, becoming more Welsh than ever in her excitement. 'Just now it's empty because the children are on holiday. I am sure my sister would be able to arrange for the school to be lent to us for a day. There is a big dining-room where we can have our dinner, and there is a play-room, too, for games, if it does happen to rain.'

'This sounds just the thing, Sister Jones,' Miss Marsden declared.

'Could we arrange for someone to cater for dinner and tea for us?' Dr Brydon wanted to know.

'Oh, yes, I think my sister could arrange that with some hotel or café. She would be very pleased indeed to help us,' Sister Jones declared.

'It's rather a long way from Milchester, but it does sound the ideal place for us,' Dr Brydon agreed. 'After all, too, the children will enjoy the journey by motor coach as much as anything. They've seen so little of the world outside Milchester for such a long time that they'll love going through all the towns and villages.'

'A long afternoon on the sands will be quite enough, too. We don't want them to get overtired,' Sister Jones added.

'We'll be going through the Mersey tunnel. *Whoopee!*' Dan exclaimed, tracing the route on the map with his finger.

'Sister Jones's plan sounds jolly good, I think, but let's do the thing in style. Will those in favour please signify in the usual manner?' Roger put the proposition to the meeting in his most dignified fashion.

Everybody held up a hand except Dan, who was still poring over the map. The rest of the meeting stared in surprise at him.

'Don't you want to go to West Kirby after all, Dan, you owl?' Simon demanded.

'Of course I do!' Dan replied indignantly.

'Then why don't you put up your hand with the rest?'

'My goodness, is that what Roger meant? Why does he want to use such long words?' Dan exclaimed in disgust. It was indeed a case of the pot calling the kettle black, but Roger ignored this remark.

'Carried unanimously,' he announced in his best manner to the further mystification of Dan, who continued to hold his hand up after the others had lowered theirs, then, finding he was alone, dropped it hastily.

'And now I propose we leave the final arrangements in the capable hands of the ladies of our committee,' Roger said, feeling that he had sustained the dignity of being chairman quite long enough – and, anyway, it was time for the cricket practice to begin. 'A week next Thursday, then,' he reminded them all, and on that the meeting broke up, and Sister Jones scuttled off to make sure that all her patients had really washed their hands before they had supper.

A week the following Thursday there was a tremendous commotion at the entrance to Beechacres, where two motor coaches were drawn up, waiting. It was a lovely sunny day, and Sister Jones was trying in vain to marshal her wildly excited flock into something like order and to make certain that everyone carried a raincoat, a bathing costume and a towel, ready for bathing or paddling. Mr Cameron came along to see if he could be of any assistance.

'Is everyone here now and quite ready, Sister Jones?'

'Oh, yes, we are indeed, Mr Cameron,' she laughed. "Everyone was up and doing hours ago. No trouble with breakfasts this morning. Oh, no! Waiting with hats and coats on for ages we've been.'

Sister Jones was besieged once more by her excited little patients. Sadie Smith's voice rose in a wail of distress. 'Sister Jones! Sister Jones! I've lost my bucket and spade. Tommy Miller's hidden them, and he won't tell me where they are.'

Sister Jones whirled round upon the grinning Tommy Miller and soon reduced him to subjection. 'Now, Tommy Miller, just you give them back to Sadie Smith at once, you bad lad! Getting above yourself, you are! Don't be a goose, now, Sadie. Stop crying. Where's your handkerchief?'

Hardly had she comforted Sadie than Katy Dollan was pulling excitedly at her coat sleeve.

'Sister Jones, must we take raincoats?' she began rebelliously but Sister Jones quelled her with a glance.

'Yes, Katy Dollan, you must. Now, don't argue.'

Clara Cox came up to Sister Jones, scowling a little, her mouth pursed up in an obstinate little pout, such as she always gave when she was determined to have her own way.

'I want to take my rabbit with me, Sister Jones. I don't want to go without my rabbit.'

'Now, Clara, you know you can't do that. You might lose your rabbit,' Sister Jones warned her.

Clara, however, was not to be denied. The pout grew even more pronounced. 'My rabbit wants to play on the sands, too,' she declared obstinately.

'Oh, dear! Now she's going to be awkward,' Sister Jones said in an aside to Dan. 'How am I to take her mind off it?'

Dan, for once, however, proved equal to the occasion. 'Put your rabbit back in the hutch, Clara, and you can take Dog Jonathan instead,' he said persuasively. There was method in Dan's coaxing.

Dr Brydon looked quizzically at him, drawing her brows together. 'I don't remember saying Dog Jonathan could come, Dan.'

Dan put forward his very best effort at persuasion. 'Oh, Mother, you wouldn't leave him behind, would you? Look how he's wagging his tail, *asking* to come. Besides, he'd love to play "Tig" on the beach with all of us, wouldn't he, Sam?' he appealed to his chum for support.

Sam rose loyally to the occasion. 'Aye, Jonathan's jolly good at fetching sticks out of the water, too, Dr Brydon.'

Marsdie could not resist putting in a whimsical plea for

82

Jonathan as well. She had a soft spot for Dan and Sam, despite all their mischief – or because of it.

'It might be absolutely necessary to have a stick fetched out of the water, Alice,' she coaxed.

'There you go, Marsdie, with your cajoling tongue,' Dr Brydon laughed, unable to resist this third plea. 'All right, then, Dog Jonathan can come, but you must keep him very quiet in the motor coach.'

'Oh, we will, we will,' Dan promised. 'Clara Cox shall hold him if she likes and let him look out of the window.'

Clara was quite pleased with this arrangement; the rabbit was forgotten, and everyone was satisfied all round.

Mrs Hallam appeared on the scene, staggering under the weight of two enormous baskets.

'Just give me a hand up with these, will you, Roger?' she asked.

'But, Mrs Hallam, we arranged for dinner and tea to be provided at West Kirby,' Miss Marsden reminded her.

'Eh, Miss Marsden, love, you get proper hungry on t'sands. I reckon a curran' bun and a drop of home-made lemonade won't come amiss.'

'Just like you, Mrs Hallam: you spoil us all.'

Mr Cameron informed them that they could all take their seats, and immediately the clamour around Sister Jones broke out afresh.

'Sister Jones, may we sit where we like?'

'Sister Jones, I want to sit next to Jessie Brown.'

'Sister Jones, where shall we put our buckets and spades?'

'Sister Jones, shall we be able to paddle as soon as we get there?'

'Sister Jones, Reggie Robinson says I've got his rain-coat – and I haven't.'

'Sister Jones, where shall we have our dinner?'

'Charlie Carter's bringing his concertina, Sister Jones.'

Sister Jones put her fingers to her ears. 'Oh, dear! Oh, dear! Do stop buzzing round me like a hive of bees, or I'll go mad. Get into the coaches everyone, please, the little ones next to the windows. Orderly now, one at a time. Roger, will you help me to get the little ones seated?'

'With pleasure,' Roger said, lifting Clara Cox and Dog Jonathan into the very seat she wanted. He looked back over his shoulder. 'Oh, Marsdie, did you bring the camera? I left it on the kitchen table at One Elm Cottage.'

'Yes, I did pick it up. Oh, dear! Now, where can I have put it?' Marsdie exclaimed distractedly.

'I saw a leather case lying on Mr Cameron's library table, Miss Marsden,' Sister Jones informed her.

'I'm near the door. I'll just nip out again and get it. Don't go without me,' Miss Marsden called over her shoulder as she disappeared down the steps of the motor coach and in the direction of Beechacres – but it is doubtful whether Roger heard her last remark.

Mr Cameron and Dr Brydon had been superintending the arrangements for seating the children in the first coach, and Dr Brydon hurried over to the second one to see if everything was ready for the start there, too.

'We're all safely stowed on the first coach. Are you?' she asked.

'Yes, Dr Brydon,' Sister Jones called from the back of the coach.

'Mr Cameron, Mrs Hallam and I will go with the first coach. Then you can follow us out of the gates.'

'Very well, Mother,' Roger called. He was busy settling a dispute between Tommy Miller and Sadie Smith as to who should have the seat by the window, and had just managed to persuade Tommy that if Sadie had the seat on the outgoing journey, he could have it coming back. He failed to notice that Marsdie had not resumed her seat in the coach, and the driver took his place, started his engine, let in his gears and clutch, and began to turn slowly out of the main gates to the accompaniment of ear splitting cheers from the occupants of the coach. Susan, however, noticed the vacant seat.

'I say, where's Marsdie?' she cried.

'She'll be with Mother in the coach in front,' Simon said.

'Then what's her coat doing on this seat?' Susan demanded, holding the garment up.

'Golly! It *is* her coat. I say, Roger, where's Marsdie?'

Roger clapped his hands to his head. 'Oh, my goodness! She went to fetch the camera. We must have left her behind. I say, driver, stop! Stop, please! We've left one of the party behind.'

With a grinding of brakes and gears, the driver pulled up. Luckily they had only got a couple of hundred yards along the road. Hardly had they drawn up when Marsdie came pounding breathlessly after them. Roger dashed to give her a hand up the steps.

'I say, Marsdie, I *am* sorry! We didn't mean it, really. The others thought you were with the coach in front, and I didn't notice you weren't in your place.'

'My!' Miss Marsden exclaimed as soon as she got her

breath back. 'What a nasty turn I got when I saw the coach turning out of the gates. Ooh! I wondered if you'd find out before you reached West Kirby, or whether I'd have to run the whole way behind you!'

'We really are frightfully sorry, Marsdie,' Roger apologized, red-faced. 'I forgot you'd gone back for the camera.'

'Well, Roger Brydon, it's a mercy you didn't forget me altogether,' Marsdie laughed. 'I've done a bit of forgetting in my time, but never as bad as that.'

'What about the time when you left a whole caravan full of Brydons behind you, Marsdie?' Susan put in slyly.

'Heavens! So I did! That's something I had forgotten, Susan.'

'What did you say you'd gone back for, Marsdie?' Simon asked, an impish note in his voice.

'The camera, of course. On Mr Cameron's library table. Here it is,' Marsdie said triumphantly, producing the case.

'Well, I'm jiggered!' Roger exclaimed.

'Why?' Marsdie demanded.

'That's not the camera. The camera was in a *black* leather case, Marsdie, not a brown one.'

'Oh, I remember! Then, what in the name of fortune have I got here?'

Miss Marsden proceeded to open the case and produced a pair of binoculars to her own and everyone else's astonished gaze.

'*Binoculars*, Marsdie! Mr Cameron's binoculars,' Simon teased her gently.

'Oh!' Marsdie exclaimed, taken aback.

'Now we shan't be able to take any snaps. What a pity!' Roger said. 'Though it was my fault in the first place for leaving the camera behind,' he admitted.

'If it's the camera you've been worrying about, Roger, then Ruth has it with her in the first coach. *She* picked it up from the kitchen table,' Susan told them.

'All's well that ends well, then,' Marsdie said with a sigh of relief, settling herself more comfortably in her seat.

'Except that you nearly got left behind for nothing, Marsdie, and it's all my fault,' Roger said ruefully.

'Not for nothing! Maybe the binoculars will come in handy – you never know,' Marsdie said jauntily. 'I like to have a pair of binoculars about me at the seaside. It makes me feel like an old salt.'

The coach rumbled through Milchester, and it seemed as if everyone in the village was standing on a doorstep to watch them go and to wave to them cheerfully.

'Now for a jolly day,' Roger said when they had finished waving back and Milchester was falling away behind them.

CHAPTER SEVEN

Marsdie uses the binoculars

DR BRYDON was quite right: the children from St Jona-than's thoroughly enjoyed their trip by motor coach. It was the first time that many of them had seen the busy workaday world since they had been sent from the big hospital of St Jonathan's in Liverpool to the small country hospital in Milchester. Some of them, whose cases had needed slow and patient treatment, had been there for a long time. Small wonder that when they reached busy Preston with its factory chimneys, they cheered. Part of their journey had wound along by the river and there was keen excitement when Sadie Smith actually spotted some swans sailing proudly on the gently flowing waters.

At Preston the coach branched off along the road which passes through a number of pleasant villages to Ormskirk. On either side the country was good flat farming land, a contrast to the hilly country of the Longridge Fells at the foot of which was Milchester. At Ormskirk there was great excitement, for there, at the side of the wide, old-fashioned street, was the open-air market. Stalls were gay and colourful with plums, pears, rosy apples, tomatoes and green vegetables. As Marsdie said, it looked like one big harvest festival. There were open-air drapers' shops, with garments hung on lines round the stalls like banners. At another stance a man stood on a box and proclaimed the cure-all virtues of a particular pill to a crowd which was amused at his jokes. Other people stood watching a woman pegging rag rugs in a gaudy pattern. A vendor of china-ware had all his stock spread out on the edge of the pavement: perilous pyramids of plates and earthenware crocks.

'Eeh, it would be awful if someone fell off a bicycle and crashed into them dishes,' was Sam Mitton's comment.

' "Blunders in China" or "Death by a Thousand Cuts".' Roger pretended to make up gruesome titles.

The coach halted for a few minutes to let the children watch the busy life of the market, and Mr Cameron got out and joined the crowd by the fruit stall, to return triumphantly in a short time with two baskets of ripe Victoria plums, one for each coach. These were a most welcome refreshment. Once more the coaches rattled on, and it was not long before they reached the outskirts of Liverpool and made their way through teeming streets to the entrance to the road-tunnel which runs under the Mersey to Birkenhead. Eager little faces were turned this way and that, and there were shouts of delight as familiar landmarks were sighted, for many of the children hailed from Liverpool. There was a momentary halt while the drivers paid the dues at the toll-house, and then on they went into the plainly marked monotonous roadway of the tunnel.

For Dan, the tunnel was something of an anti-climax, for he had expected a sudden descent into inky darkness, illuminated only by the headlamps of the coaches, and this well-lit roadway seemed rather ordinary. Sam Mitton, however, was entranced.

'Eh, man, think of all that weight of water up above –

and maybe there are ships sailing over us right now.' His eyes grew big. 'It's a wonderful job of engineering. When I grow up I'm going to build tunnels like this one,' he declared.

'If I remember rightly it was big dams and reservoirs you were thinking of when we were in camp, Sam. Didn't you and Dan try to build a dam in the river there to hold the fish in a pool?' Roger teased him.

'Aye, but 'appen I can build dams as well as tunnels,' Sam replied quite seriously, taking both in his stride. 'Big stuff, anyway, Roger. I mean to do it,' he vowed quite determinedly.

Soon they emerged into the sunlight again and left Birkenhead and its suburbs behind; then by way of pleasant villages and roads lined sometimes by green hedges and sometimes by modern pretty houses, they reached the seaside near Hoylake, and in a very few minutes more were at West Kirby and drawing up before the Westgarth School. Here Sister Jones's teacher sister was waiting to greet them, so very like Sister Jones that Mrs Hallam declared they must be twins; and almost before one had time to blink one's eyes, the happy party was out of the coaches and seated in the dining-room at a most appetizing dinner. It was amazing how very hungry everyone was; but then, breakfast had been early and most people had been too excited or too busy to eat.

For a time nothing much was heard save the clatter of knives and forks, dishes and spoons.

'Now, could anyone else eat a second helping of pudding?' Dr Brydon asked.

The pudding was a really marvellous pear trifle, with sponge cakes, dates, sultanas and custard, and with – yes –

cream too on top, so that it was small wonder that plates were passed up so fast that it took Dr Brydon, Mrs Hallam, and Sister Jones all their time to deal with them.

'*Second* helps, indeed, Dr Brydon!' Sister Jones exclaimed. 'Charlie Carter, have you any room for a *fourth* helping?'

'Not if I'm to run you out at cricket on the beach later on, Sister Jones,' Charlie retorted with his impish grin. 'Only that thought holds me back from having two more helpings.'

'No cricket till everyone's lunch has been down for half an hour at least,' Dr Brydon said decisively. 'No, Sister Jones and I are going to spread out ground-sheets under those trees in that lovely shady garden, and then the young folk from St Jonathan's can lie down for a short rest before we go down to the beach.'

'Oh, gosh! Do we all have to have an after-dinner nap, Mother?' Dan asked, looking rather put out about it.

'Well, perhaps we'll say everyone under eleven years old,' Dr Brydon conceded.

'Oh, good! That cuts out Sam and me and Charlie and Juan. What a lucky thing I've just had my eleventh birthday,' Dan cried, dancing about in excitement. 'May we go down to the beach, Mother?'

Dr Brydon hesitated: Dan had such an aptitude for getting into unexpected scrapes! But the beach was clean level sand, and the tide was out.

'Better let them go, Dr Brydon,' Sister Jones whispered. 'If they stay here they'll just make all the little ones fidgety to be off and they ought to have a quiet rest.'

'Perhaps Charlie should stay,' Dr Brydon began, but

Charlie looked at her with such a heart-rendering expression that she stopped short.

'Oh, have a heart, Dr Brydon. I'm as strong as a plough-boy now,' he pleaded.

'Very well, then. Only, remember, all of you – no mad rushing about,' Dr Brydon cautioned them.

'Don't worry, Dr Brydon. I'm saving myself to lick Sister Jones at cricket,' Charlie informed her. Sister Jones shook her fist at him in a mock threatening fashion.

'And *no bathing*, mind,' Dr Brydon went on, forgetful that the tide was far out. 'We'll have an organized bathe later on at the bathing-pool, with Miss Marsden and Roger to act as safety patrols.'

'Oh, splendiferous!' Dan said.

'Proper champion!' was Sam Mitton's verdict.

'Then we'll go and mooch round the beach a bit and throw stones for Dog Jonathan till you're all ready for a game,' Dan proposed. 'Are you coming, Marsdie?'

Miss Marsden shook her head. 'No, I think I'm going to climb Grange Hill instead – there won't be time after tea. That's that nice heathery hill just behind the town. I'm going to use those binoculars now I've brought them, and I'm going to look for ocean liners leaving the Mersey on their way to America.'

'I'll come with you, Marsdie, if you'll have me,' Simon offered. He always enjoyed a ramble with Marsdie, and they often quested for things of historical interest together.

'Gladly, Simon,' Marsdie beamed at him. 'Anyone else coming?'

'Yes, I'll come, Marsdie,' Susan replied. The twins were never far away from one another on an expedition.

'Too energetic for me after a meal, Marsdie,' Roger excused himself.

'Lazy crittur, Roger!' Miss Marsden said, tweaking his ear. 'What about you, Ruth?'

'I've promised to read a fairy tale to the very little ones while they rest. Perhaps I'll meet you on the way back,' Ruth suggested.

'Right! Come along, Simon. Ready now, Susan?' Miss Marsden prepared to go.

'Oh, Marsdie, what big eyes you've got!' Roger said in a parody of Red Riding Hood.

'What do you mean, Roger? Not that I'm the big bad wolf, I hope?'

'No – just that your eyes must have telescopic lenses if they're going to pick out those ocean-going liners far across the sea. But then, you are an old salt, aren't you?' he teased her.

'Roger Brydon, what are you getting at?'

'Merely that you're leaving behind those Beeootiful Binoculars on that chair.'

'Bless me! So I am!' Marsdie cried, returning to pick up the binoculars. 'Thanks, Roger. After nearly getting left behind because of them, I ought to make some use of them now. Come on, Simon. Let's see if we can be up that hill in twenty minutes. Wait for that bathe till we get back. We shan't be long,' she promised.

Out on the sands Dog Jonathan was having a wild time running round in circles while the four boys threw pebbles for him to fetch. At times when two of them threw pebbles at the same moment, he rushed undecided between one and the other, sometimes halting midway between and looking from one boy to the next, with his paw in the air and a ridiculous pleased expression on his face while he panted for breath. This was Jonathan's idea of a doggie's paradise. The boys tired of the game long before he did.

'Golly, what a lot of sand!' Dan exclaimed, looking about him. 'It stretches for miles. If we've got to wait for the tide coming up, it's going to be a long time before there's even enough water to wet our ankles.'

'I think there's a swimming pool further along the beach where Dr Brydon intends us to go for our bathe,' Sam reminded him.

'Then there was no need for Mother to forbid us to bathe here. There isn't even enough water to paddle in,' Dan declared.

'Oh, I guess the tide comes up pretty quick along them channels,' Charlie gave his opinion in his clipped Cockney tongue.

Juan was gazing into the distance. 'Are those leetle islands out there?' he asked.

'Yes, they are. At least, they would be islands if the tide was up,' Dan qualified his statement. 'It looks as if we could walk out to them now across the sands. I wonder if we could.'

'There's a man just coming across the sands with a horse and cart now. Let's run across and ask him,' Sam suggested.

'I wonder what he's doing with a horse and cart right out on those sands,' Charlie wanted to know.

Juan eyed the wide expanse of sands rather doubtfully. 'There will not be any queek-sands, you think?'

'Nay, Juan, not if a horse and cart can cross them!' Sam pointed out with his customary common sense.

They set out to run towards the approaching horse and

cart. As they drew up level with it, Charlie, full of curiosity, tried to peep in the cart.

'Say, mister, what have you got in that cart?' he asked with an irresistible grin.

'Cockles, mi lad, and a few good crabs,' the man replied. 'Take a look, lads,' he said good-naturedly, stopping his cart.

'Did you get them out there?' Dan asked with interest.

'Aye, I dig t' cockles out o' t' sand banks at low tide. They're only buried two or three inches down. That's why I tek this spade wi' em. And these 'ere crab pots I set at t'other side o' the islands. I teks 'em out at low tide and sets 'em i' rocky pools , then waits a tide and fetches 'em back again.'

'What do you call those islands?' Dan asked.

'Well, t' biggest' un wi' the coast-guard station on it is called Hilbre. Then t' middle 'un is Little Hilbre. It's got nowt but one or two sheep grazing on it and yon little island wi' the iron basket on a pole for fire-signalling is called the Eye.'

'Ooh! Do people signal by fire now?' Sam asked, much impressed.

The fisherman shook his head. 'No, though folk do say it was used at the time of the Armada, but I reckon that's just a tale. The iron basket wouldn't have lasted all these hundreds o' years, not wi' salt spray blowing o'er it.'

'Can you get out to the islands without a boat?' Dan inquired.

'O, aye, if you don't mind getting your feet wet. You'd have to splash through a few channels. The deepest one is near the island. It's called the Gutter. The tide runs proper fast up it.'

'Could we *paddle* out to the islands, then?' Dan asked.

'Yes, I reckon you could, if you watched for t' turn o' t' tide. There's not much time, mind, and the water runs up fast. Lots of folk picnic at Hilbre. A nicer spot you couldn't find, but folk mostly wait a tide and spend the day on the island. They wade out one low tide and come back the next low tide. It needs a fine day like this for it, for there's not much shelter on the island.'

'Are there any caves, Mister?' Charlie put in eagerly.

'Aye, there's one or two. It's said that sailors used to smuggle brandy and other liquors into 'em, and about a hun'erd years ago the landlord of an inn on t' shore here made his fortune out o' smuggled brandy from Hilbre.'

'Oh, I say!' Dan exclaimed with eyes big with excitement.

'Well, I'd best be pushing on.' The fisherman gathered up the reins again. 'Got to get mi crabs boiled for market. So long! *Tck! Tck!* Come up, Betsy.'

With a nod of his head and a wave of his hand, he set off over the sands in the direction of West Kirby.

Charlie gazed wistfully towards the islands. 'Coo, I would like to see them caves!'

' 'Appen there's smuggled treasure in them yet. You never know,' Sam wished hopefully.

'Let's wade out and see,' Dan suggested at once, but the others hung back a little.

'But Dr Brydon said we were not to bathe,' Juan reminded Dan of his mother's words.

'But this isn't bathing, Juan. This would be wading,

paddling, you know. Mother didn't say we couldn't paddle, did she?'

'But what if t' tide comes up quick?' Sam demurred.

'Well, we shall see it coming up, shan't we?' Dan argued. 'If the channels seem to be growing deeper we can turn back.'

'Perhaps we ought to ask Dr Brydon first?' Charlie said doubtfully.

'It might be too late to see the caves if we go back to Westgarth, Charlie. Oh, come on, get your shoes and socks off and tie the laces and sling the shoes round your necks. Then we'll run for it and see if we can get to the islands before the tide comes up.'

'All right, mi 'earty.' Charlie came over all nautical. 'Coo, I'd like to see them caves!' He began to caper round, singing,

> 'Fifteen men on the dead man's chest,
>   Yo-ho-ho and a bottle of rum.'

'Oh, come along, make haste,' Dan cried impatiently, whipping off his own shoes and socks. 'Whistle up Jonathan.'

Jonathan, who was scratching busily in the sand after an imaginary rabbit in an imaginary rabbit burrow, was only too happy to chase alongside them, with an occasional scamper ahead towards the islands. As he splashed through the shallow channels between them and Hilbre, he barked with sheer delight.

*   *   *

Miss Marsden, Susan, and Simon stumbled up the last

sandy little lane towards the summit of the hill. It had taken them rather longer than they had expected, for it was a harder climb than it had looked from the promenade of the little town.

'Goodness, Susan, what a scramble!' Marsdie exclaimed, as soon as she had breath enough to speak.

'Gosh! I'm out of breath, too,' Susan cried.

'I begin to think old Roger is wiser than we imagined. It is a bit of a pull up on top of that large dinner Sister Jones's sister arranged for us,' Simon agreed.

They turned and looked over the roofs of the town out to the blue sea and the shimmering haze beyond. The view amply repaid all their efforts in the climb.

'Oh, how lovely it is, now we are at the top,' Susan exclaimed. 'Look at all the tawny brown bracken and purple heather around us. What lovely colours! And the cluster of roofs below us, then that golden stretch of sand fading into that blue-violet sea. The sunshine makes it look almost tropical.'

Simon struck an attitude and recited:

'Dear old West Kirby,
Nestling down so calm,
Thine air is bracing and thy breath is balm.
Sites contend for fame, but truth must e'en allow,
The laurel wreath to thy heather brow.'

Marsdie gazed at him in astonishment. 'Good gracious, Simon, you're a poet!' she declared.

'Oh, I can throw off a little thing like that on occasions,' Simon said modestly. Susan, however, was laughing at him and gave him a sisterly little push.

'Get away, Simon! You read that bit out of a guide book before we left home.'

'So I did!' Simon admitted with a grin, quite unabashed. 'A pity you knew about it, or I might have gone on basking in poetical glory to the end of time. But, I say, Marsdie, what about those binoculars you've cherished all the way from Milchester for this great moment. Let's have a look for those big ships a-sailing to America.'

'Here we are!' Marsdie took out the glasses. 'We shan't have time for more than a look-see before we've to scramble down and join the bathing-party.' She adjusted the glasses to her sight and looked far out to sea. 'Yes, there is a big liner going down to the bar, I think, but there's a hazy kind of mist and I can't distinguish it awfully well. Take a look, Simon.'

Simon scanned the seas in turn. 'There are a few cargo boats and a couple of dredgers, too, Marsdie. The Mersey's a busy river, isn't it?'

'Let me have a peep,' Susan said, anxious to take her turn. Simon passed the binoculars to her. 'Oh, don't they bring everything beautifully near,' she cried. 'It only looks a hop, skip and jump to those enchanting little islands. What do you call them?'

'The Hilbre Islands,' Marsdie told her.

Susan focused the glasses on them. 'I can see the coastguard's house plainly, and I can even distinguish the sheep grazing on that middle island.' Suddenly she gave a cry of surprise and consternation. 'Oh, I say!'

'What is it, Susan?' Marsdie asked anxiously.

'Those four little figures running across the sands and wading through the channels – I'm sure they're some of

99

the boys. They look like Dan and Sam and – yes – Charlie and Juan, too. Look, Marsdie.'

She passed the glasses to Marsdie who looked hard at the diminutive figures.

'I believe you're right, Susan. One figure seems to limp slightly, as Charlie does. But you have a look, Simon. Your eyes are keener than mine.'

Simon looked long and carefully. 'Yes, that's Dan and company all right,' he gave his verdict. 'I can see Jonathan, too, splashing through the water with them. Mother did say they might roam on the sands, of course. They're quite near that island now.'

'I do hope they turn back soon,' Marsdie said anxiously. 'The tide has a way of running in very quickly along those channels.'

'Yes, Marsdie, you're right. The tide should have turned by now, I think. It was pretty low when we arrived at West Kirby. I hope they don't linger about on the island. Dan's a silly little donkey at times,' Simon said, a little troubled too. He continued to look for a moment through the binoculars. 'Oh, my goodness!' he exclaimed suddenly.

'Oh, what's the matter?' Marsdie clasped her hands in alarm.

'Sorry, Marsdie, I didn't mean to startle you, but that misty haze well – it's blotted out the cargo boats and dredgers completely. It's creeping up to the land. If it reaches the island the boys might go wandering in circles over those sands when they try to come back to the shore. They might really be caught by the tide.'

There was no disguising Miss Marsden's alarm now.

'Oh dear! We must do something at once. And here we

are, practically a couple of miles away. What *can* we do?'

'We'll have to tear down the hill and run across those sands and fetch them back just as quick as we can,' Simon made a rapid decision. 'It'll mean wading, Marsdie. Are you game? There's no time to go to Westgarth first, either, to tell Mother and Mr Cameron.'

'Susan, *you'd* better go to Westgarth and tell them what's happened and what we're doing. Don't alarm anyone, because quite likely we might meet the boys on their way back; but tell Mr Cameron quietly that if we're not back soon, all of us, it might be as well for him to arrange for a boat to bring us off when the tide rises.'

'Right, Marsdie,' Susan promised.

They began to scramble down the hill as hard as they could. As they ran, Marsdie panted, 'We *must* get to those boys before the mist reaches the islands and the tide cuts them off.'

CHAPTER EIGHT

Adventure on the island

THE four boys, headed by Dan, made good speed towards the largest island of the group, Greater Hilbre. Jonathan, his tail wagging wildly, ran in circles about them over the firm hard sand, or splashed gaily through the shallow channels after them. These channels cut deeply into the sand in several places, winding about between the mainland and the islands. The sand embankments were often steep and undercut by the race of the tide, but the water in their beds was nowhere more than two or three inches deep, until the boys reached the last and deepest channel of all, the one mentioned by the old fisherman as the Gutter. The boys scrambled down its bank eagerly, for this was the last barrier between them and the island.

The water, however, was deeper than they expected. Jonathan was soon out of his depth, though this rather added to his enjoyment of the whole expedition, and he swam joyously across on the dog paddle, his muzzle held well above water, in the wake of the wading boys. Dan found that his feet sank in the rather oozy sand in the bed of the channel, and he had to stop to hitch up and roll the hems of his navy shorts, as the water reached his thighs.

As he scrambled breathlessly up the further bank and on to the sloping, rock-strewn beach that led to the island, he cried, 'I say, that last channel was a bit deeper than I expected. I've rolled my shorts up but they've got a bit wet.'

Charlie Carter regarded his shorts rather ruefully too. They were considerably more soaked than Dan's, as he had blundered into a deeper pool in the rather uneven channel.

'Mine are wet too,' he announced. 'I guess Sister Jones will have something to say about it when I get back, if she notices them.' Charlie stood just a little in awe of Sister Jones.

Juan gave a chuckle. 'The fisherman said people called that channel the Gutter. You'd better tell Sister Jones you slipped in the gutter.'

'Not much use when there's been no rain for days,' Charlie said despondently.

'Well, we've reached Hilbre Island at last,' Sam said, surveying the low rocky cliffs and the short green grass above them. There was also a coast-guard's white-painted house with a red roof and other out-buildings, surrounded by a rough fence. 'Look! There's a short stone jetty stretching out from the side of that little sandy cove there, and sloping down towards the Gutter.' He indicated.

'That'll be where the coast-guard brings his boat in. He's got to get all his groceries and supplies from the mainland, you know,' Dan informed them with an air of authority. 'See, he's got his boat pulled up there just above high-water mark.'

'Then that will be his house overlooking the cove, but I don't see anyone about,' Juan said, scanning the fenced enclosure of the house and look-out cabin.

'Oh, come on, we haven't come to look at coastguards' houses. Let's find those caves and explore them,' Charlie said impatiently.

Sam laughed at Charlie's eagerness. 'Goodness, Charlie, to hear you talk, you'd think you were going to stub your toes on some half-buried treasure the minute you got inside the cave!'

'Laugh if you like, Sam Mitton,' Charlie replied indignantly, 'but I'm all for searching.'

Charlie's home had been in the East End of London before he came to St Jonathan's, and smugglers' caves had certainly not been a feature of the drab, endless rows of streets, all dingy and alike. This island was entirely a new thing in his experience, and it was small wonder that the Cockney lad's active imagination had been fired by the old fisherman's yarns. Sam and Dan did not wish their friend to be too badly disillusioned if no treasure were forthcoming.

'I'm afraid these caves 'll have been searched many a time, Charlie. People often come across here, so the fisherman said. There doesn't seem to be anyone about just now, but that may be because it's a bit late for picnic parties when September comes in.'

'I think the cave must be on the other side of the island, facing the sea. It can't be far round this little rocky bay,' Sam surmised.

They plodded on round a miniature headland and across the little shallow bay, till they came to a kind of rocky spine which ran right from Greater Hilbre to the very small island known as the Eye. Juan stopped to survey this rocky ridge.

'There's a chain of rocks joining the big island to the

little one,' he said. 'It should be quite easy to explore all the islands from this one.'

'If there's time, we will,' Dan promised easily.

Sam was not so much taken up with the possibilities of exploration as with the interesting marine life he found in the little rocky pools. In one of them a jelly-fish had been stranded by the out-going tide.

'Eh, look, there's a purplish kind of jelly-fish in this pool,' he shouted to the others. The boys came running to look.

'Coo! I ain't ever seen a jelly-fish before,' Charlie announced, deeply interested. Even Dog Jonathan sniffed curiously at this strange sea beast, but was too cautious to examine it more closely.

'Don't poke it, Charlie. I've heard people say they sting,' Dan warned him.

'Lift that stone, Dan,' Juan directed, indicating a very large rounded pebble on Dan's side of the pool. There was a quick movement and something hid itself hurriedly in a crevice between the rocks.

'I thought I was right,' Juan said triumphantly. 'There was a crab under that stone.'

'It scuttled sideways like a big yellow spider,' Sam exclaimed.

'I guess there are lots of shrimps and little fishes in these pools. I wish we'd brought shrimping-nets,' Dan said regretfully.

'Eh, Dan lad, we wouldn't have time to go shrimping.' Sam Mitton gave his opinion with his usual practical common sense. This brought them back sharply to the business in hand, that of exploring the cave. They continued their journey along the north-west shore of the island, till, all of a sudden, after rounding another little headland, they came on the cave. Charlie rushed in first, then stopped short, a little taken aback.

'It's not as big as I thought it would be,' he said disappointed.

Dan peered about in the gloom at the end of the cave. It fell short of his expectations, too.

'No, there aren't any winding passages leading from it that I can see. All true smugglers' caves should have winding passages where they hid their ill-gotten gains.'

' 'Appen the passages have got blocked up wi' sand and falls of rock,' Sam Mitton suggested with his practical mind, seeing that both Charlie and Dan were reluctant to relinquish their belief in possible treasure. 'Mebbe the smugglers used those ledges high up to hide their brandy bottles.'

'Hi! Gimme a leg up and I'll have a look,' Charlie said at once. Dan and Sam supported him while he made an inspection of the rocky ledges.

'No, not even a bit of broken glass left – only this scrap of dried seaweed,' he exclaimed in disgust.

'Well, let's have a look along the rest of the island,' Dan said, giving up the idea of finding treasure in the tide-washed cave.

They strolled out into the sunlight again, scrabbling with their toes in the wet sand.

'There are some very pretty pink shells here,' Juan said, stooping to pick up one or two delicately marked ones. 'I wonder if Miss Marsden could thread them like beads and use them for her handwork class.'

'Or Sister Jones,' Charlie hailed the idea. 'She might

not be so mad at us for getting a bit wet if we took some shells back for her.'

'Let's each pick a few – as many different kinds as we can,' Dan proposed.

They searched diligently along the beach, filling their pockets, blissfully unaware of the flowing tide. Nearer and nearer the sea crept to the island, but for the boys time was out of mind. Suddenly a splashing wave near his feet woke Sam Mitton to the realization that the tide was coming in fast. He straightened himself from his hunt for shells and shouted to the others.

'Look! Isn't the sea a lot nearer than it was? It's reached that rocky point near the cave.'

'Gosh! So it has,' Dan cried. 'Perhaps we'd better be going back.'

Juan looked out to sea beyond the point of rock. 'Oh! I can't see the Welsh coast on the other side of the estuary. There's a mist creeping up over the sea,' he cried in dismay.

They were all thoroughly alarmed by now, and Sam Mitton, at least, was fully alive to their danger.

'Come on, chaps, let's make for West Kirby as fast as we can, before we're cut off by the tide,' he urged them.

Round the rocky end of the island they rushed, splashing in places through the oncoming, though still shallow sea, slipping and stumbling over the damp sea-weed, making a better pace over the firm sand of the tiny bays. At length they were back on the side of the island facing West Kirby, and they plunged down towards the deeply-cut 'Gutter'.

'Here we are. Once we're over this we shall be all right,' Sam declared.

Dan looked askance at the swiftly running stream. 'It looks a bit wider than when we came, doesn't it?'

'And a bit deeper,' Charlie added ruefully, trying the depth of the water step by step. 'Sister Jones will have something to say if we go back drenched to the waist!'

'Yes, she'll make us take off our clothes and sit wrapped around in blankets while the rest of the folk play at cricket or go swimming,' Juan predicted gloomily.

Dan was wading with caution into the stream and the water was mounting quickly up the calves of his legs.

'Heavens! I'm up to my knees already, and I'm not a quarter of the way across – and it's much, much deeper in the middle. The channel's twice as wide as it was, too.'

The boys all looked at each other in dismay. Another step would plunge them in right up to their thighs, and in the middle the current ran fast, with enough strength to sweep a badly-balanced wader off his feet. While they had been gathering shells, the tide had swept round the island and along the channel like a river in spate.

'It 'ud take us up to our middles at least,' Charlie groaned. The certainty of Sister Jones's wrath drew much nearer. Sam Mitton tried to find a practical way out of their difficulty.

'Mebbe we've struck the channel at a fresh place where it's wider and deeper. We're nearer the north of the island than we were when we first came across, I think. There must be *some* shallow places, like fords, in a river. Let's work back to the south, along the edge of the stream and keep trying it till we reach a place where we *can* cross.'

This seemed sound advice and they hastened to follow it. Every few yards they tested the depth of the channel, but the result was always the same: there was no place where they could wade across comfortably.

'Too deep here,' Juan reported, after trying a few steps with his longer legs.

'Let's try it here,' Charlie urged, at a place where the bank did not seem so steep. 'No,' he cried hastily, drawing back from a kind of step in the sandy bank that would have plunged him well in: 'it 'ud take us up to our waists at a few strides.'

'It'll be shallower down there, I think,' Sam said hopefully, pointing to a fresh place about fifty yards farther on.

'Yes, you're right, Sam,' Dan said, rushing once more into the water, 'it is shallower.' Then he gave a dismayed little shout as the water suddenly submerged the roll-up of his shorts. 'No, it isn't shallower – at least, only for a yard or two, and then it shelves very steeply. Gosh! Are we never going to get across?'

'Even Dog Jonathan seems a bit bothered, and he can swim,' Juan said rather unhappily.

Jonathan gave a little whine, as if to agree with this, and ran hesitantly a few yards along the bank and towards the water, then back again to the boys, looking up inquiringly at them.

'We seem to be coming to a rocky bit,' Sam announced. 'Perhaps we could jump across from rock to rock. Come on.'

The slimy nature of the lichen-covered rocks made jumping difficult, and they had to pick their way slowly.

'We must look like a lot of goats playing "Follow my Leader".' Juan could not help giggling.

Dan, however, did not feel like laughing. Things were

growing far too serious, and he was perturbed because it was his fault that they had come to the island, and he knew that he had not kept faithfully to the letter of his mother's instructions. The first thin wreaths of sea mist began to swirl and billow about them. Distances grew deceptive.

'There's a mist coming down. Don't go so fast, Sam. I can hardly see you in front,' Dan shouted to Sam, who was leading the way.

Charlie looked around him, feeling somewhat disconcerted, too.

'The mist's coming between us and the mainland. We won't know which way to go soon, if we don't move more quickly.' That, however, was not very easy over the slippery rocks.

Sam called back reassuringly, 'It's all right. I'm coming to sand again. It's a sand-bank, so we must have crossed that beastly channel after all, somewhere among these rocks. Come on. The sand is fairly smooth. We'd better run.'

Charlie and Juan laboured over the remaining rocks.

'Don't go so fast, Sam. Remember, I've still got a bit of a game leg,' Charlie called.

'So have I. Take it easy,' Juan cautioned him, too.

'I say! We're coming to *grass*!' Dan, who had just caught up with Sam, cried in utter stupefaction.

'*Grass?* But we shouldn't be reaching grass yet,' Sam exclaimed, and this time a little note of anxiety sounded in his voice, too. 'There should be nearly a mile of sand before we come to the sand-dunes at West Kirby.'

'Stop a minute. I can hear something. It sounds over there,' Charlie said.

With dismayed and rather fearful faces the boys looked at each other and listened. Queer, sharp, rasping sounds came from a few yards away. Rather timidly they advanced in the direction of the sound.

'There it goes! It's a *sheep*!' Juan cried.

Sure enough, a sheep shied away from them and trotted off to be lost instantly in the fast-gathering mist.

'A sheep! Then we're nowhere near the mainland at all. We must have crossed the rocks to the other island, Little Hilbre,' Sam deduced rapidly. 'That means we're still as far from the shore as ever.'

'Oh, golly!' Dan groaned. 'Then we've still got that awful channel to cross.'

'We'd better find the channel as quick as we can and wade through it, no matter how wet we get, before the tide rises any higher, or we might be here all night,' Charlie cried, becoming rather desperate.

Sam was looking about him in bewilderment. 'Puzzle, find the channel now in all this mist,' he said.

'I think it's down there. Listen! You can hear the tide running up it,' Dan said, pointing in the direction he judged to be the right one.

There were unmistakable sounds of the water rushing in waves up the channel. They listened in silence for a moment.

'Yes, you can hear it coming up fast enough,' Charlie said ominously. 'That channel 'll be nearly four feet deep by now.'

'Well, we can all swim a stroke or two, except Juan, and I think Sam and I could manage to pull him through with us, one on each side. We shouldn't have to swim more than a couple of yards, at the worst. Come on,' Dan said, willing to chance it; but Sam held him back.

'Nay, Dan, the current's so strong you might get carried along by the tide. Besides, it might be more difficult to tow Juan through the water than you think. Remember, we've all got our clothes on and we're not used to swimming fully dressed. Clothes can get frightfully heavy in the water. I've got a better plan than that. Let's go across the rocks the way we've come, back to the other island. The coast-guard's got a house there, remember, and he's got a boat. Perhaps if we ask, he'll ferry us across that deep channel and we'll just have to wade through the other smaller ones between us and the shore.'

'That's a good idea, Sam,' Juan applauded, feeling uncertain of his possible performance in the water and of Dan's ability to tow him. This certainly was the safer plan.

'The coastguard might lend us a compass, too, to find our way once we'd crossed the channel. We'd be really adventurers then.' Dan was of an incurably optimistic and romantic mind.

Sam was beginning to clamber back over the rocks in the direction they had come. He stopped after a yard or two, however.

'As far as I can remember, this is the way, but we'll have to go slowly. It might be as well to put our shoes on again. These sharp rocks fairly hurt your feet.'

The others agreed with him and a halt was made while they donned hose and shoes once more.

'Mind you don't slip on the seaweed. There are one or two awfully deep pools,' Juan said.

'Aye, Juan, and they seem a bit deeper than they were,' Sam replied apprehensively.

Suddenly there was a slight splash followed by a shriek.

'Is that you, Charlie? Are you hurt?' Sam cried, turning back at once to help him.

'No, I'm not hurt,' Charlie assured him. 'But I've slipped between two rocks at the edge of the pool, and I've got my foot wedged.'

'Oh, dear! Can't you get it loose, Charlie?' Dan asked.

'No. I'm doing my best, but I just *can't* get it out,' Charlie answered, tugging hard at his foot, and trying at the same time to maintain his balance by holding on to Sam.

'Eh, this is a bit of a bother,' Sam said, decidedly worried. 'Pull harder, Charlie.'

'I can't. It's not a bit of use. It's held as tight as if it were in a trap.'

Juan was surveying with horror the water in the pool below. 'The tide's coming up fast. You can see the water rising in the pool. It's pouring in through all those crevices.'

Charlie went pale. Fear began to clutch at him.

'We'll have to do something. Let's try if we can shift this smaller rock,' Sam said.

The other three boys heaved and strained and tugged at the rock, but it was too firmly wedged in place and much too heavy for them to stir.

'It's not a bit of good. That rock must weigh a ton at least,' Juan gasped.

'Let's all try pulling at Charlie. His foot went in the

crack. It'll just *have* to come out,' Dan suggested desperately.

This new effort had no effect beyond making Charlie wince with pain.

'Oh, stop! Stop!' he cried. 'It hurts horribly. It will only end in spraining my foot or pulling it out of joint and it'll be wedged in just the same.'

'This is awful,' Juan exclaimed, frantic with anxiety.

Sam threw a sober glance at the oncoming tide and the ever-deepening pool. 'Aye. The waves are slopping over into the next pool already.'

Charlie pursed his lips grimly together, and the corners turned down for a moment, almost as if he were going to burst into tears. But Charlie was tough. He turned very pale, but he said quite firmly, 'You'd better go and save yourselves. It's no use all of us being drowned.'

To leave Charlie was the last thing the others would have dreamed of doing. They began to think desperately of other means to free him.

'Maybe if one of us could get across to the big island and get hold of the coastguard quickly and bring him to help –' Dan began, but Sam cut him short.

'Too risky. We might not find the coastguard at once, and the tide might have risen a lot before we get him over here to Charlie. Wait! I've got a notion. I'm going to take off my shorts and shirt and go down into that pool and see if I can get Charlie's shoe off, or cut it away, or something –'

'I see what you mean,' Juan said quickly. 'We can't get at it from above, but we might get at it from below.'

'That's right. And the water in the pool isn't too deep for me yet, though it will be soon,' Sam said, stripping off his clothes quickly. 'Cheer up, Charlie. We shan't leave you and we'll soon have you out.'

Sam gave his clothing to Juan to hold, while Dan supported Charlie, and then he slipped little by little into the pool, gasping at first at its coldness, and stretching out his feet to feel how far away the bottom of the pool was from him. In a moment he was standing on a level piece of rock, with his head and shoulders well out of the water and just level with the rock crevice in which Charlie's foot was wedged.

'I can just manage. It's not too deep yet,' he said, reaching up with his open clasp-knife. 'Now, Charlie, when I've cut the shoe-lace loose, try to turn your foot round in the shoe. Hold on to him, Dan, while he wriggles round.'

Sam slipped the blade of his knife under the shoe-lace and cut it apart. Charlie immediately tried to wriggle his foot round in the shoe.

'It's coming round a bit now, but not enough,' Charlie cried. 'Help me to twist it round to the right, Dan.'

'Wait. I can slit the leather a bit across the top of the foot,' Sam said, hacking away with an upward cut of his knife so as not to injure Charlie's foot. 'Now twist round again and pull. Go on, lad. You're doing fine. Your foot's coming out. Pull again.'

Charlie struggled manfully as Sam directed him, and suddenly, like a cork from a bottle, his foot came out of the shoe and he was standing on his two feet beside Dan, free once more. It was then that tough Charlie almost wept for joy.

'Thank goodness you're out, Charlie!' Juan exclaimed in heartfelt tones.

'Thank Sam Mitton that I am!' Charlie declared equally fervently from the bottom of his heart.

Sam was busy trying to detach the shoe from its securely wedged position, but without any luck. Just then a rather larger wave sent a wash of water over the edge of the rock into the pool. The water rose perceptibly. It was clear that another few waves like that one would raise the level of the water in the pool to the surrounding rocks upon which they were standing.

'Come out, Sam, do, before you're submerged,' Dan cried shrilly, fearful for his chum.

Sam saw the sense of this and reluctantly began to lever himself out of the pool with Dan's help.

'I reckon you'll have to leave your shoe behind, Charlie,' Sam said, giving a backward glance at the pool and unwilling to give up the attempt to rescue the trapped footgear.

'Coo! What will Sister Jones say? I'll have to hop for the rest of the day, too, now I've only one shoe. Still, there's no help for it.'

'Better your shoe than your foot, and perhaps yourself as well, Charlie.' Juan reminded him of the danger he had just escaped.

Sam was busy trying to dry himself as best he could with his own handkerchief and those of his three friends. As quickly as he could, he put on his clothes over his shivering little body. Warmth began to come back into him again.

'Got my belt, Juan? Right.' Sam girded himself. 'All set now. Let's make a bee-line for the big island.'

Once again the four boys resumed their slippery journey from the middle island to Greater Hilbre.

CHAPTER NINE

A strange apparition

As the boys began to scramble back over the rocks towards
Greater Hilbre, Juan peered this way and that. The mist
had now entirely surrounded them.

'Which way do we go from here?' he asked. 'I can't see
the big island now.'

True enough, Greater Hilbre had disappeared behind a
white blanket of mist.

'I think we should work slowly in this direction. Watch
your feet, everyone. Now, take care and don't slip again,
Charlie.' Sam took command of affairs once more.

The boys picked their way gingerly over the green,
mossy rocks, holding on to each other while Sam led the
way. Every few yards there were now deep pools round
which they had to skirt. Suddenly Sam stopped.

'Wait a minute. We've come to a wide gully between
the rocks,' he announced. 'It's a bit too wide to chance
jumping across it and the foothold's too slippery, anyway.
We'll have to work round it. Bear right, all of you.'

Cautiously they picked their way round to the right,
still holding on to each other. All at once Charlie gave a
cheerful shout.

'I think we're across at the other island. Here's the sand
again.'

'And here's the grass, too,' Juan said, but he was a little

puzzled. 'Shouldn't we have climbed some low cliffs before we come to grass?'

'Look! There's a sheep. I suppose all sheep are alike, but that's the twin of the one we saw before,' Dan remarked with some misgiving.

'I didn't see any sheep on *Greater* Hilbre,' Charlie commented.

Sam stopped dead. The awful truth had dawned upon him. 'That big rock there is the very one we started from. We've just been working in a big circle in this mist. We're back on *Little* Hilbre again.'

The boys all stared gloomily at each other.

'At this rate we shall never reach the other island and the coast-guard's house,' Dan said despondently.

'It looks like it,' Sam admitted in tones of deep gloom. 'It took rather a long time to get you out of that crack, Charlie, and I reckon the sea will have come up too far now to let us get across the rocks to the other island in all this mist. We can't see our way properly, and, like as not, we're already cut off by the tide.'

'Yes. The islands are separated when the tide comes up. You can tell that by the seaweed over the rocks,' Juan pointed out.

'I'm afraid we'll have to wait on Little Hilbre till the tide goes down again,' Sam told them.

'How long will that be?' Dan inquired.

'A – about eleven or twelve hours, I believe,' Sam faltered unhappily.

The boys looked aghast at each other.

'Why, that will be the middle of the night and it will be too dark for us to see our way across by then,' Dan exclaimed.

'Perhaps someone will come and fetch us off with a boat,' Charlie said hopefully.

'But no one knows we're on the islands,' Juan reminded the others.

It was too true, they thought: they had come across in such a hurry, they had told no one where they were going, and Dan knew in his heart of hearts that this had been lest Dr Brydon should forbid the excursion.

'Sister Jones and everybody will be worrying about us, too,' Charlie said remorsefully.

Sam, with his practical mind, began to think out how they could make themselves comfortable on Little Hilbre, till someone discovered them, or till the tide went down again.

'I think the best thing we can do is to see if there's any building on the island like the coast-guard's house on Greater Hilbre. There might be a boat somewhere, too.'

At this suggestion the others began to take fresh heart.

'Yes, we'd better explore as much as we can in this mist,' Dan agreed. 'At least we might find some sheltered place, if we've got to spend the night here.'

'It would be as well to keep close together,' Charlie warned them.

Juan suddenly seized Charlie by the arm. 'Stop talking! Listen! I thought I heard someone *cough* just now.'

The boys instantly froze into silence. Then, from a short distance away, came the unmistakable sound of a half-stifled cough.

'There *is* someone on the island besides ourselves,' Dan exclaimed with relief. 'Perhaps it's a fisherman with a boat.'

They all began to call out, 'Hi, there!' 'Where are you?' 'We want help.' 'We're caught by the tide.'

Their shouts died away. There was no answer, not a call in reply. The white mist cloaked the velvety silence. A little fearful, the boys looked one to another.

'No answer! That's a rum go,' Charlie said, voicing everyone's thoughts. 'I'm certain someone coughed.'

'Perhaps it was a sheep. They do cough sometimes,' Sam suggested as a possible solution.

Juan shook his head. 'It didn't sound like a sheep, and I know all the noises animals make, from the days when I was with Braddock's circus. Listen! There it is again.'

There was once more a sharp cough, followed by a sneeze which could be neither stifled nor prevented.

'It must be a man. He *sneezed*.' Charlie cried, 'Hullo, there! We're over here. Can you find us? We want help. Please come over here.'

They waited for the sound of footsteps coming to them, but no sound came. All was eerily, uncannily silent, as before.

'It's very q-queer – as though someone didn't want to answer,' Dan said.

'Perhaps he's deaf,' Sam hazarded as a guess.

Dan suddenly pointed to their right, where there was a momentary gap in the mist.

'Look! Look quickly! There, where the mist is thinning a bit. Isn't that a man standing there?'

'It is, an' all! Hi, mister!' Sam cried to the hazy, rather frightening figure, which, however, did not move in their direction. It seemed to be holding a weapon, as though threatening them.

Once again the mist began to swirl about them and

between the boys and the strange apparition there was again a white, foggy blanket through which it was impossible to see. Almost it seemed as though the figure had been a trick of the mist, and the boys might have been inclined to believe it that, but for evidence of the cough and sneeze.

'He's gone! Oh, bother it!' Charlie cried in despair.

Juan's sharp ears had caught another sound, however. 'Listen! He's running away.'

Sure enough, dulled though the footfalls were by the short turf, they seemed to be in rapid retreat, and once there came the sound of a stumble and a muttered exclamation.

Dan gave a little nervous shake. 'It – it's a bit *ghostly*, isn't it: a man looming up like that out of the mist and then disappearing?'

'Eh, Dan, ghosts don't sneeze,' Sam Mitton said with his hard-headed common sense. 'But it is proper queer, all the same. He must have seen us, too, when we saw him. Why did he want to slip away like that?'

The others shook their heads. 'I don't like it a bit,' Juan said. Suddenly the island had assumed a sinister aspect to them all.

'We'd better go on exploring, but we'll all stick together, I think,' Sam said soberly.

'Yes, let's,' Dan agreed.

'I've got a sort of horrid feeling that I want to look over my shoulder all the time – as though there's someone or something following us,' Charlie faltered, taking a furtive peep over his right shoulder.

Juan gave a low whistle to bring Jonathan to heel. He felt safer with Jonathan beside him. Jonathan, however, kept making little divergent circles in the mist, with a nose for a possible rabbit.

Suddenly Dan gave a little shriek. 'Oh, what's that?'

'Just a sheep, Dan,' Sam reassured him.

'They come up out of the mist like horrid white shapes with black faces,' Dan said unhappily.

They plodded on, feeling their way step by step over the unknown and unseen ground before them.

'There seems to be nothing but rocks and grass. It's not going to be a bed of roses if we've got to spend the night here,' Charlie sniffed a little.

Juan gave a little shiver. 'Ugh! I feel cold already.'

'Shipwrecked mariners always light a fire with driftwood,' Dan said, full of romantic notions as ever.

'Got any matches?' Charlie asked him practically, and then, when Dan shook his head, remarked with some irony, 'I thought as much!'

Dan relapsed into an unhappy silence for a few moments.

'Listen! I think there *is* someone following us,' Juan said.

They all stood still in their tracks. 'No, it's only another sheep cropping the grass over there.' Juan was able to interpret the sounds to their relief.

'If only this mist would lift, we might be able to make signals to the shore,' Sam said with a sigh.

'The other folk must have missed us by now,' Charlie said. All at once he gave a slight stumble into a concealed hollow in the ground. Sam's hand shot out at once to steady him.

'It's all right. I just stumbled into that hole. I'm not hurt,' Charlie assured him.

Juan was busy examining the hole. 'It looks like a trench, as though someone has been digging here,' he remarked.

Sam scrutinized the hole with him too. 'Aye, it's not so long ago either. That soil has been freshly turned over,' he gave as his opinion.

'Why should anyone want to dig on this island?' Dan asked, but no one was able to supply him with a satisfactory answer.

Sam looked about him, then pointed to a little hollow in the shelving ground running down to the seaward shore. 'What's that little building down there in the shelter of that rock? It looks like a small shed.'

The mist had thinned slightly again, enough to show them that they were indeed only a few yards from a little wooden shed, almost concealed by the big rock against which it was built.

'If we can get into that shed it will at least give us shelter if we've to stop the night here,' Charlie said.

'There might be a boat in it,' Dan suggested hopefully.

'Nay, it's too small for a boat, Dan,' Sam pointed out.

They had now reached the shed and found that a door on the other side of it was open. They looked inside.

'Someone keeps tools here. Look! There's a spade and a riddle. Who would want those on this island?' Charlie asked.

'The person who dug that hole, most likely,' Sam said with his practical judgment. He peered farther into the hut. 'It looks as if he sleeps here. There are two dirty-looking grey blankets in that corner.'

'And a mug and a tea-pot and some bread and cheese

on that shelf,' Charlie pointed out, too. 'At least we shan't starve if we have to stop the night here.'

'It must be that man we saw for a moment who is digging on the island. I wonder what he's digging for?' Juan said, puzzled.

'Perhaps he's digging for gold,' Dan said, his eyes opening wide. 'Maybe he's found a gold mine on Little Hilbre that no one knows about.'

'Or a buried treasure, maybe,' Charlie added, not to be outdone by Dan's imaginings, and his mind still dwelling on possible smugglers' loot. 'You know, that fisherman did say that once smugglers used to come to these islands. I'm sure it's a buried treasure,' he declared loudly.

'Yes, it *is* a buried treasure, but none of you spies will get it!' a sepulchral voice cried outside the hut. There was a quick slam of the door, a turn of the key, and the boys found themselves imprisoned in inky darkness. The suddenness with which it happened left them speechless for one brief moment, then they burst into a chorus of angry and frightened cries.

'Hi! Who slammed that door?' from Charlie.

'We're locked in!' Juan exclaimed in consternation.

'Eh, let us out!' Sam shouted.

'It's just someone playing a silly joke,' Dan declared.

They banged hard at the door but it remained obstinately shut.

'Bang away!' the hollow voice mocked at them, followed by a cackle of crazy laughter. 'Knock as hard as you like. There's no one on this island to hear you. Come after my treasure, would you? I'll teach you a lesson. Spies! That's what you are. Spies after my treasure!' The voice rose to a pitch of demoniacal rage.

'We aren't! We know nothing about any treasure. Let us out!' Dan shouted back.

'Oh, yes, you do. I heard what you said about gold and buried treasure. I heard it all,' the voice replied. 'You're spies, but you'll never get at my treasure. Never! Never!' Again came that wild crazy laugh.

'Now, mister, lay off it. You know quite well we're nothing but a bunch of kids caught by the tide.' Charlie tried to reason with the owner of the voice. 'All we want to do is to get back to the mainland. Let us out of this.'

'No. There you are and there you'll stop,' they were told.

'How long are you going to keep us here?' Juan demanded.

'As long as need be. Perhaps days – weeks – months – till I've found my treasure and got safe away with it.'

Dan, with just a little quaver in his voice, exclaimed, 'Why, we should starve to death!'

'Yes, slowly. That's the end spies deserve . . . spies sent by the police to watch me. But you'll be *thirsty* first. He, he! You'll be thirsty first,' the voice gloated over them.

Charlie clutched at his own throat and swallowed hard. 'Coo, I'm thirsty now!' he muttered to the others.

'Eh, mister, you can't do that to us. Let us out, or you will get into trouble with the police,' Sam shouted boldly.

'I knew you had something to do with the police,' the man said triumphantly. 'I'll teach you to come after my treasure. *My* treasure!' the man replied. Once again he laughed in hideous fashion.

'I think the chap's clean crazy,' Charlie cried.

'Let us out! Let us out, I say! Let us out!' Dan began yelling, and he banged with his fist on the door at the same time.

'Bang away! Shout away! No one will ever hear you here,' the voice mocked him. Once more came that burst of frenzied laughter, but this time the sound of it began to die away in the distance.

'He's going away and leaving us locked up here,' Juan cried in alarm.

They redoubled their bangs on the door and their shouting for help, till they were hoarse and their knuckles were sore; but when they stopped there was only silence.

'It's no good. We're too far away for anyone to hear us. This hut muffles our voices and the sound of the waves crashing over the rocks is too loud. We'll just have to sit here and wait till someone visits the island,' Sam said with resignation.

'That won't be until the tide is out again tomorrow,' Charlie said dismally.

'Maybe that fisherman will come across then,' Dan hoped.

'Or maybe the folk from St Jonathan's will start a search party. They'd never go back to Milchester without us. I hope they think of these islands,' Juan added.

'Coo! I'd even be glad to see Sister Jones right now,' Charlie said, meaning it.

'We shall have to keep shouting from time to time. Someone's sure to find us,' Sam observed with greater certainty than he really felt.

'Yes, if our voices don't become too weak,' Dan sounded rather despairing.

Charlie began to feel all round the walls in the darkness.

'If only there was a window anywhere, but there doesn't seem to be.' All at once he stumbled over the spade leaning up against the wall of the hut. 'Here's the spade,' he cried.

'Let's try tunnelling under the wall of the hut,' Sam suggested.

They felt round at all the likely places and lifted a spadeful or two of sand off the floor, but they soon came to solid rock after they had scraped two or three inches of sand away.

All at once Juan asked, 'I say, where's Jonathan?'

'He was with you last, Juan. You whistled him to heel, remember,' Dan reminded him.

'He's not always a very obedient leetle dog,' Juan said sorrowfully. 'He's not here now, anyway. Oh, do you think that crazy man can have done something to him?' Juan was desperately anxious.

'But Jonathan wasn't with us when we came to the hut. I'm certain of that, or he'd have gone sniffing about the way he does,' Sam argued.

'That's right, Sam. And Jonathan would have barked at that fellow when he shut us up – perhaps even have gone for him – and he didn't.' Charlie carried the argument further.

'Where is the dog, then?' Juan asked anxiously.

'I bet he's gone rabbiting. He's a terror for going after rabbits when they're not in their cages. That's what he'll have done. Mebbe he's down a rabbit-hole somewhere now, this very minute,' Charlie strove to reassure Juan.

'Let's whistle for him,' Dan said.

'No, no! I wouldn't do that,' Juan spoke quickly and apprehensively. 'That man might be lurking about outside, and if he saw Jonathan he might do him some injury.'

Sam was quick to approve Juan's common sense. 'Juan's right. It's no use getting Jonathan into trouble as well as ourselves. The only thing to do is to wait a bit and see what happens.'

Feeling most desperate and unhappy, they sat down on the floor of the hut to wait.

CHAPTER TEN

Marsdie goes in pursuit

HURRY as they might, Miss Marsden, Susan, and Simon found that it took them longer than they had expected to reach the winding road at the foot of Grange Hill and then to take the way through the little town to the beach. They emerged on the sand at a point nearly a mile from the place where the St Jonathan's party had elected to have their games on the shore and where already the wicket had been set up. Miss Marsden, however, decided that there was no sense in wasting precious time by joining the main party, but she sent Susan instead to tell Dr Brydon and Mr Cameron what they had seen through the binoculars at the top of the hill, and to let the rest of the party know that she and Simon were going in search of the boys. Marsdie scanned the expanse of sand but without sighting Dan and his friends.

'Oh dear! I can't see any sign of the boys. I hoped they'd have been on their way back by now,' Marsdie gasped, still rather out of breath.

'They must be still on the islands, or we should have seen them returning. I say, Marsdie, it's an awful long way across,' Simon said.

'And the tide must have turned by now,' Miss Marsden could hardly keep the anxiety out of her voice. 'I wish I knew for certain whether they are still on the islands. I wonder if anyone has seen them.'

'Perhaps those men talking by that cart over there could tell us something. I'll ask them,' Simon volunteered. He strode across the sand to where a horse and cart were drawn up near a stony slope from the beach to the road above. The horse stood patiently while a fisherman in a blue jersey argued at length in friendly fashion with two other fishermen. Simon approached them.

'Excuse me, but did you see four boys go across to the islands some little time ago?'

'Four lads about twelve or thirteen years old? One of 'em limped a bit, and they had a dog wi' them?' the fisherman asked.

'Yes,' Miss Marsden said eagerly. By now she, too, had joined the little group.

The fisherman nodded his head. 'Aye, about an hour past there were four of them paddling out towards the islands. They stopped and chatted to me – asked me a lot of questions, they did. But I thought they were only going a part of the way towards the island.'

'You haven't seen them come back, have you?' Miss Marsden asked.

The fisherman thought hard and then shook his head slowly. 'Come to think, I haven't, and I've been here talking with Bill and Tom a goodish while. Those lads must be still on Hilbre. Eh, and the tide's turned and 'll be coming up fast. Unless they're across it already, they'll not get across yon deep channel, the Gutter, now,' he added in sudden alarm.

'Oh dear! I hope they don't try to cross now. Look! There's a mist coming up. It's beginning to blot out the islands already,' Miss Marsden exclaimed anxiously.

'Aye, if they don't know the landmarks they might easily wander round and round in circles and get trapped by the tide on one of them sandbanks.' The old fisherman was quick to appreciate the danger.

Miss Marsden clasped her hands nervously. 'Oh, we must do something at once. We'd better run across to the islands as fast as we can, Simon. We'll have to take our shoes and stockings off.'

Miss Marsden was beginning feverishly to unlace her shoes when the fisherman laid his hand on her arm.

'Wait a minute, missus. *You'll* not get across that big channel, the Gutter, either. It lies close to the island and it's the first to fill, so the lads will probably be still on the island as you can't see 'em crossing. You might even have to wade through a couple of feet of water in the shallow channels by now. I'll tell you what. I'll take you in my cart as far as the Gutter. It'll be too deep to take you across it, but 'appen you could shout to those little lads from there and tell them to stay where they are.'

'Is there no way of getting them off the island?' Miss Marsden asked, rather taken aback at the prospect of a delayed return to Milchester for the whole picnic party.

'Aye, if we can make Mr Thomas – the coastguard, he is – hear us. He's got a boat and he might be able to ship the youngsters across the Gutter and I'll pick 'em up in the cart. Come on, missus. Climb in over the wheel. There's no time to be lost.'

'Oh, thank you, thank you,' Marsdie said, putting her foot on the hub of the wheel and, assisted by Simon, clambering into the cart. 'This is awfully kind of you.'

'Eh, we can't see young lads risk their lives trying to

cross the Gutter on a rising tide, missus. Come up, Betsy.'
He gave a hitch and a flick with the reins at his patient old
mare. '*Tck! Tck!* Hurry up, lass.'

The mare began to move as quickly as her rather unwieldy frame would allow, and even essayed a kind of
half-gallop, half-trot, which shook and bounced the cart
and made it sway from side to side, with Miss Marsden
clinging rather perilously to its side and to Simon. Now
hastening, now slowing down when they came to a channel, they wound their tortuous way across the sands, for
the fisherman had to ford the channels where they were
shallowest and where the banks were not too steep for the
cart to mount at the opposite side. Sometimes the water
rose within a few inches of the hub of the wheel, and Miss
Marsden realized that it would have been impossible for
her and Simon to have crossed the channels without getting their garments soaked. At last they reached the swifter
running tide of the 'Gutter', where already the water was
beginning to lip and brim over the edge of the banks and
would soon begin to flood the sand flats between the channels. As they approached, the mist over the islands drifted
out towards them and began to envelop them.

'We're at the Gutter now, missus,' the fisherman told
them, 'and the island's across yonder, though you can only
see it as a dim shape. Aye, the channel's too full to get
across, and I reckon your young lads won't be able to see
us either, in this mist. You'd better shout for them.'

Marsdie and Simon shouted at the tops of their voices.
'Dan! Sam! Boys, are you there?'

There was no answer. Simon made another attempt to
make them hear. 'Dan! Da-an! Are you boys on the
island? Charlie! Juan! Where are you?'

Miss Marsden called too, but the only reply they got was a faint echo from the low cliffs nearby.

'There's no reply,' Simon said, giving up at last. 'Oh, Marsdie, you don't think they've started to cross already and they've been swept away by the tide and – and –' Simon faltered, unable to go on, for the thought was too horrible to contemplate.

'Oh dear, Simon!' Marsdie exclaimed, very much upset. The fisherman attempted to cheer her up.

'The lads may be on one of the other islands, missus, and if they are, they won't be able to hear you for the noise o' the sea. We'll try shouting for Mr Thomas, the coast-guard, I think.' He raised his voice. 'Mr Thomas! Mr Thomas! It's me, Jim Hughes. Mr Thomas, are you there?' When there was no immediate reply he said to Simon, 'You shout too, young chap.'

Simon and Miss Marsden joined him in a shout at the tops of their voices. 'Mr Thomas! Mr Thomas!'

After a few minutes during which they continued their combined effort, a voice from the island came to them through the mist.

'Ahoy there! Who's shouting? Does anyone want me?'

'It's me, Jim Hughes, Mr Thomas, sir. Have you seen anything of four lads on the island?'

'Four lads? No, but I've been behind the house working in the vegetable garden. I might easily have missed them in this foggy weather. It came down so quickly. Are you sure they're on the island?'

'I saw 'em start off for it, Mr Thomas, and there's a lady wi' me who's looking for 'em, and she saw them through her spy glasses almost on the island, and they haven't come back, or we'd have been bound to have seen 'em.'

'Yes, I saw them through my binoculars splashing through the Gutter. They belong to our picnic party at West Kirby, and they have a dog with them. I saw them before the mist closed in.'

'We've been shouting for 'em for quite a bit,' Jim Hughes added.

'Then they ought to have heard you shouting if they're on this side of the island, anyway. Wait a minute. I'll bring the boat across to fetch you and we'll make a search of the island.'

In a minute or two they heard the sound of a boat being dragged down the sloping beach to the water and launched; then the sound of oars and rowlocks, and a few seconds afterwards the boat, with Mr Thomas in it, emerged out of the mist and made straight for the high bank of the channel where they were standing. It happened that this bank had been cut almost vertically by the race of the current, and when old Jim Hughes got down from the cart and steadied the boat against the side of the bank, Miss Marsden was able to step directly into it, helped by Mr Thomas's strong hand. Simon followed her into the boat, and straight away Mr Thomas began to pull back again towards the little jetty on Hilbre.

'I'll wait here wi' the cart, missus, to take you back o'er the sands,' Jim Hughes called after them.

When they reached the farther bank the coast-guard jumped out first, saying, 'Give me your hand, ma'am, and make a jump for the jetty.'

Miss Marsden did so and, as soon as she was safely ashore, Mr Thomas asked Simon to help him to give the boat a pull up on the shore, so that the tide would not wash it away. This done, Mr Thomas led them up a cliff path and made to walk right across the island to the shore on the west side which faced the open sea.

'We'll strike right across here to that cave on the other side of the island,' he told them. 'We'll see if they're playing about there. Caves have always got a fascination for youngsters.'

As they scrambled down the rocky path on the farther side, they shouted again for the boys, but there was no reply. When they reached the cave, it was empty, with the tide almost reaching it. It would have been impossible to walk round the island now, for both the rocky points which enclosed the little bay were under the rapidly rising tide. Mr Thomas very closely scrutinized the strip of sand just at the mouth of the cave.

'Those footmarks show that there have been two or three people round the cave and that they had a dog with them,' he announced as his findings. 'The lads have been here all right, but there's no sign of them anywhere near just now. We'll call them again, though, to make sure.'

Once more Miss Marsden and Simon made the echoes ring with their shouts, but there was no reply.

'I don't think they're on Hilbre, ma'am.' The coast-guard shook his head. 'But I'll tell you what I'll do. We'll go back to the boat and I'll row you along the Gutter, and we'll see if they're on the other islands.'

'Thank you so much. I feel dreadfully worried,' Marsdie said, her anxiety growing with every minute.

They followed Mr Thomas back to the boat and Simon helped to launch it again. As Mr Thomas took the oars, he called to Jim Hughes through the mist, 'Hi, Jim! The lads are not here. I'm rowing down the Gutter to Little Hilbre to search there. Follow us along the bank of the channel as close as you dare.'

'Aye, aye, Mr Thomas,' came back to them from the farther bank, as Jim Hughes lifted the reins and urged the patient Betsy on once more along a course parallel with the Gutter.

'It won't take long. It's only about four or five hundred yards along to the cove on Little Hilbre where I can beach my boat,' the coast-guard assured Miss Marsden. He pulled away with a will and then, although the outline of Little Hilbre only appeared ghost-like at intervals through the swirling banks of mist, he unerringly headed the boat for the particular part of the shore where he wanted to land. It was a small, cup-shaped cove, from which it was easy to reach the little plateau of grass on the top of the island.

'Here we are,' he said, as the boat grounded. 'Help me to give the boat a pull ashore, will you?'

Simon and Miss Marsden both gave him a hand to haul the boat up.

'That'll do nicely. The tide won't float her off from there for a while yet.'

They climbed up easily to the top of the low, grassy cliffs.

'This is a much smaller island than Greater Hilbre. Shout hard, and the lads 'll be bound to hear you, if they're here.'

Again Marsdie and Simon shouted for the boys, but there was no reply save for the melancholy cries of the sea-gulls and the boom of the waves against the rocky spine which united the islands at low tide. Marsdie once again raised her voice despairingly. Mr Thomas was beginning to shake his head doubtfully when an idea suddenly came to Simon.

'Marsdie, the boys had Jonathan with them. Let's whistle. Jonathan's ears are quicker than their's. He's bound to come if he's on the island at all. Let's give his particular whistle.'

Simon gave a perculiarly piercing whistle by putting the first two fingers of his right hand to his mouth and blowing two notes, one low and one high and shrill. Twice he did this and then, in the distance, from the other side of the island, came an answering bark. Simon repeated the whistle. It was followed by a succession of barks and yelps of delight, coming ever nearer and nearer.

'He's here! Jonathan's here!' Simon cried.

'Then the boys can't be far away,' Marsdie said with renewed hope.

Like a cannon ball projected from a gun Jonathan shot at them over the turf. Wild with delight, he jumped up at them again and again, trying to lick their hands, their faces, in an orgy of affection at having found them.

'Good dog, Jonathan! Take us to Dan. Where's Dan? Where's Sam?' Marsdie cried, as excited as Jonathan.

Jonathan ran back a few steps as though he understood and wanted them to follow him. To make his meaning clearer he came back to Marsdie and whined, a little beseeching note.

'I think he wants us to follow him,' Simon said.

'Come on, ma'am. We'll go after the dog,' Mr Thomas decided.

'Oh, but why don't the boys come themselves? Why

don't they answer when we call?' Miss Marsden asked in an access of new fear.

'We can only follow Jonathan and find out, Marsdie.' Simon urged her on.

They followed the little dog right across the middle of the island towards the opposite coast.

'He seems to be taking us straight across to the other side. That's where the old diggings were,' Mr Thomas remarked.

'Diggings?' Simon asked with interest.

'Yes. A university professor, with a few students and two or three labourers, began some excavations on the islands for traces of the early British, whom they thought might have had a fort here.'

'Did they find anything?' Simon wanted to know. History always had a great fascination for him.

'Not much,' Mr Thomas replied. 'A few bits of earthenware pottery and bronze axe heads, and one or two other such things. Enough to show that the island had been occupied in very early times, but no big discoveries.' Mr Thomas looked ahead after Jonathan. 'Ah! I thought so: your dog seems to be going towards the old hut where the diggers' tools used to be kept. I'd clean forgotten about that little hut when we were on the other island.'

Jonathan began to caper madly round the hut, barking and yelping wildly. Simon, Miss Marsden, and Mr Thomas broke in a run towards the hut.

'There's someone in that place, I'm sure,' Simon said. 'Jonathan's going mad. Give a shout, Marsdie.'

Together they shouted, 'Dan! Sam! Are you there? Charlie? Juan?'

In reply there came glad shouts and a fusillade of bangs

on the hut door. Cries were heard: 'It's Marsdie!' 'And Simon!' Then, after those first glad shouts of recognition, came shouts for help.

'Marsdie! Simon! We're here. We're locked in the hut. Let us out, please.'

'All right, Dan,' Simon answered his brother. 'Mr Thomas, the coast-guard, is with us.'

Mr Thomas ran forward to turn the door handle, but the door failed to open. He began to search round for a key.

'The door's fastened right enough. Are you sure there isn't a key inside?' he called to the boys.

'No. The man on the island locked us in,' Dan called in explanation.

'The man on the island?' Mr Thomas cried, amazed. 'There's no one on the island! But never mind that now – the thing is to get you out of here. Now, how can we do it?' He began to look round for a weapon with which to force the door. Simon began to hunt round, too.

'Look! Here's a spade left near the diggings,' he cried, running with it to Mr Thomas.

Mr Thomas regarded it with astonishment. 'Now, who's been using that? There's fresh earth on it. But we'll find out about that later on. Give it here, son. It's the very ticket to do the job.' He shouted to the boys inside the hut. 'Now, you boys there, stand back. I'm going to stick the spade between the door and the framework and lever the door open.'

He inserted the blade of the spade in the crack and pressed the handle with all his might and main round to the right. There were splintering sounds, then suddenly the door gave way and the crack widened. 'That's done it!' he cried.

In an instant the door was flung open and the boys dashed outside, almost weeping with delight at being free again.

'Marsdie! Marsdie! How *did* you find us?' Dan cried, catching her by the hands.

'I saw you through the binoculars crossing to the island, and we followed you as quickly as we could, because we knew the tide was coming in. We couldn't get here fast enough to beat the tide, though, because we were at the top of Grange Hill. Mr Thomas here, rowed us over from the big island, and Jonathan found us and guided us the rest of the way,' Miss Marsden explained breathlessly.

'But whatever possessed you all to come over here?' she was beginning to inquire when Mr Thomas interrupted her.

'Just a moment, ma'am, please. What I want to know is how they came to be fastened up in this hut?'

'There's a crazy man loose on the island, mister. He kept saying we were spies come to steal his buried treasure,' Sam Mitton informed Mr Thomas.

The coast-guard opened his eyes wide. 'Treasure! There's no treasure on the islands. But did you say he locked you in here?'

'Yes – slammed the door and locked us in,' Charlie told him.

'Mm! And there was a spade in that old trench. Let's take a look at it.' Mr Thomas strode over to the trench and began examining the ground very closely. 'Why! Someone has been digging here!' he cried in astonishment.

Just then the mist parted and an evil-looking face

glared at him from a distance of only a few yards. Half-hidden behind a low rock, a sinister figure crouched, a large stone in his hand. Juan happened to look up and catch a glimpse of him.

'Look! Look! There he is, peering at us from behind that rock.'

Mr Thomas ducked at once and the stone passed harmlessly over his head and crashed on the ground behind them.

'Hi, you! Come here,' Mr Thomas called, and ran a few steps towards the rock, but the man had disappeared as if by magic. 'He's run off, but I saw him all right. I know that face. The man's name is Dawson, and he worked at the diggings before the war. Why has he come back here?'

'Perhaps he came across something valuable and buried it again, meaning to dig it up again later on.'

'Nay, nay,' Mr Thomas laughed at the idea. 'Bronze axe-heads and bits of pottery are only valuable in the historical sense. Dawson would hardly go the length of locking up these lads to hide that.'

'He said we were spies sent by the police to look for his buried treasure,' Dan told Mr Thomas.

'Oh, he did, did he? Mm! Well, I've got a kind of notion the police might be interested in him and his buried treasure. But there's no need to worry. He can't go far while the tide's up, and before it goes down again the police will soon have him rounded up on this little island.'

'How will you let them know, Mr Thomas? Will you come back to West Kirby with us in the cart?' Simon asked.

'No need for that. I've got the wireless telephone at the coast-guard station, and I can talk to the police at Birkenhead; and as soon as there's enough depth of water, the police will come straight here in a motor-boat. But the thing now is to get you all back to the mainland. Jim Hughes will be anxious to drive over the sands while his cart can still cross the channels. We'll give him a whistle to let him know we're coming.'

From across the Gutter came an answering whistle.

'He's waiting there now. Come along. We'll go back to the boat and put you across to the other side of the Gutter.'

Willing hands helped to launch the boat once again, and in a very short space of time the little party were all aboard. As Mr Thomas pulled them over to the opposite bank he said, 'When I get back to Hilbre, I'll put a call through to your friends to let them know you're on the way back.'

'We're very grateful indeed to you, Mr Thomas. You've saved us from a terrible anxiety – perhaps from something worse,' Miss Marsden said with gratitude.

'It's very little I've done, ma'am, and it's a part of my duty as coast-guard, you know,' Mr Thomas replied modestly.

'Mr Thomas, will you *please* let us know what happens to that man Dawson, and if there really *is* a buried treasure on the island?' Dan begged.

'Righto, young nipper.' Mr Thomas grinned good-naturedly. 'I'll promise you that. Where are you staying in West Kirby?'

'The Westgarth School. But we're going back home tonight. Please write to "St Jonathan's, Beechacres, Milchester,' will you? Here's an old envelope with the address on it,' and Dan proffered it.

'Thanks, but I hope I'll have some kind of news for you before you reach home. Well, here you are, across, and yonder's Jim Hughes. Don't wait now. Jim'll have to make it pretty fast as it is, to cross the Mid-Channel, but he'll just do it if some of you run alongside till you get to the channel. Hurry, now.'

The party disembarked with all speed and splashed through the shallows to the waiting cart. Already the water was beginning to lap round Betsy's patient feet.

'Up you get, missus.' Jim Hughes held out a helping hand to Miss Marsden. He noticed Charlie Carter in vain trying to conceal his limp, which had been rather more troublesome since he had wrenched his foot in the crack between the two rocks and lost his shoe as well. 'Perhaps those two lads had better come in the cart, too.' He indicated Charlie and Juan, and Simon helped them up beside Marsdie. 'The rest of you can run beside Betsy till we reach the Mid-Channel and then I'll take you all in the cart and ferry you across,' Jim Hughes directed.

'Right you are, Mr Hughes, and thanks a lot,' Simon said.

With a chorus of good-byes to Mr Thomas, the party set off for West Kirby and the rest of the picnic party. As they rumbled along, Charlie Carter thought rather unhappily of Sister Jones and the wrath to come when she discovered that one of his shoes was missing.

CHAPTER ELEVEN

Dawson's secret

On a firm, level stretch of sand just south of the Red
Rocks, a headland stretching out into the tidal waters of
the estuary of the Dee, the St Jonathan's picnic party had
pitched their wicket and an exciting game of cricket was in
progress. The low, misty breeze, which had crept up the
estuary from the sea, had not extended as far as the shore
at West Kirby, upon which the sun was still shining. Sister
Jones and Roger had chosen sides for the game.

At first there was much speculation as to where Dan
and the other three boys could have gone; but when Miss
Marsden, Susan and Simon had also not returned, Dr
Brydon concluded that the seven of them were all together
and that very likely the four boys had accompanied Miss
Marsden to the top of the hill. Roger was disappointed
that Miss Marsden had not yet returned, for she was a
very good slow bowler and he had counted upon her to
take some wickets for his side. Simon, too, was a useful
member of a team. When the missing players did not
appear, however, Dr Brydon decided that they had better
get on with the game, as some of the party also wanted to
have a quick bathe before tea. Sister Jones's teacher sister
obligingly took charge of the very small patients who were
too young to play cricket, and organized a sand castle
competition out of range of the cricket match.

Soon the game was in full swing, with Mr Cameron as umpire, Dr Brydon and Sister Jones batting at opposite ends of the wicket, and Roger bowling. Dr Brydon stepped out bravely to tackle the googly ball which Roger sent down to her, and caught it a resounding smack, which sent it well towards the sand dunes.

'Well hit, Dr Brydon! Run! Run!' Mr Cameron exhorted her, so full of admiration for this mighty hit that he forgot his role of umpire.

'Come on, Sister Jones. Put your best foot forward. Don't have me run out,' Dr Brydon shouted at her.

Sister Jones only just managed to reach the wicket before Ruth returned the ball to Roger, who sent it crashing among the stumps.

'How's that, Mr Umpire?' he cried in triumph.

'Not out!' Mr Cameron gave without the slightest hesitation.

'Well!' Roger exclaimed, flabbergasted at this decision, while Sister Jones pulled a face at him. 'Our umpire never will give the St Jonathan's side out. I'll have to do something about it. You wait, Sister Jones,' he threatened her laughingly. His opportunity for revenge came a short time afterwards, when, Dr Brydon having scored another run off Katy Dollan's bowling, Sister Jones stood up at her wicket opposite Roger once more. Roger shook his fist threateningly. 'Sister Jones, I'm going to clean bowl you this time. Look out!'

'Indeed to goodness, it's quite shaky you make me feel,' Sister Jones declared with a grin, though she was really not in the least disconcerted.

'Fee, Fi, Fo, Fum! I smell the blood of a Welsh wum*mun*,' Roger improvised.

When the swift ball broke near the wicket, Sister Jones stepped out to it and gave it a most terrific swipe right in the middle of the bat. It soared in the air and seemed to disappear, 'almost as far as Sister Jones's native Wales,' Dr Brydon afterwards declared.

'Gosh! She's hit it a mile!' Roger cried in surprise.

'If you hadn't been feeling shaky, the ball might have reached the top of Snowdon, Sister Jones,' Mr Cameron teased her.

'Fee, Fi, Fo, Fum! – to you, Roger Brydon,' Sister Jones chipped him gaily.

'It's no good: I must be off my game,' Roger said in disgust. 'Come along, young Tommy Miller. You're on our side, aren't you? Have a shot at bowling Dr Brydon.'

Tommy Miller was nothing loath. With lips pursed together and in his eye a fierce light of determination to bowl Dr Brydon, he took his run at the wicket and delivered a ball with a great deal of spin. Dr Brydon misjudged her stroke, caught the ball with the tip of the bat, and sent it straight up into the air.

'Ooh! She's hit it right into the sky. It's a catcher!' Tommy Miller cried in delight. 'Look out, Mrs Hallam!'

Mrs Hallam was acting as fielder at point, having come into the team 'just to oblige' and to take the place of the absent Simon.

'Catch it, Mrs Hallam, catch it!' all Roger's team chorused.

Mrs Hallam looked rather horrified, as if the ball descending upon her were a bomb. Gladly she would have dodged and left the ball to take its course, but something held her rooted to the spot. Down, down towards her the ball came, inescapable. Mrs Hallam gazed up at it, fascinated, her eyes nearly popping out of her head. The cry of 'Catch it!' rang in her ears. She put up her hands almost in an act of self-defence, then, completely knocked off her balance, staggered backwards.

'Gosh! She's caught it. No, she hasn't. Heavens! She's sitting down backwards on the sands. Oh, she's down! But oh, good, I say! – she's still clutching the ball! Oh, well caught, Mrs Hallam!' Roger cried, rushing to her assistance at the same time as Dr Brydon, who dropped her bat and went to help Mrs Hallam to rise. Mrs Hallam still sat in a state of stupefaction on the sand, looking at the ball in her hands as if it were a meteor from another world.

'You're not hurt, are you, Mrs Hallam?' Dr Brydon inquired anxiously, helping her to her feet.

'Eeh, not a bit, love. And I *caught* it!' Mrs Hallam exclaimed in amazement at her own achievement. 'Eeh, I never thought I could land a catch like that, not in all mi born days. Dan and Sam should have been here to see it,' she said with regret.

'Yes, where can those boys have gone?' Dr Brydon wondered as she dusted the sand from Mrs Hallam.

'Perhaps they're with Miss Marsden and Simon and Susan taking a look round the town,' Mr Cameron surmised, having come up at that moment. 'They'll be very vexed when they find they've missed the cricket.'

'That's what I can't understand —' Dr Brydon was beginning to say when Tommy Miller pointed to a figure running towards them over the foreshore.

'Look! Look! Here's Susan coming.'

Dr Brydon ran to meet her, anxious lest any calamity had befallen one of the party.

'Why, Susan, what's the matter?' she cried.

Very breathlessly Susan managed to deliver Miss Marsden's message.

'Marsdie and Simon have gone across to Hilbre Island to fetch the boys back,' she gasped.

'Hilbre Island! To fetch the boys back?' Mr Cameron repeated after her in surprise.

'Yes, Marsdie looked through her binoculars and saw them crossing the channel to the island, and she's gone to fetch them back before the tide cuts them off.'

'Oh dear! I hope they're in no danger,' Dr Brydon exclaimed instantly.

'Marsdie said you were not to worry, but just to go on with your game,' Susan told her.

'But whatever shall we do, if they are cut off?' Dr Brydon demanded, visualizing all kinds of possibilities.

'Don't worry, Dr Brydon. If necessary, I'll get a boat to bring them off when the tide rises. They're sensible lads, and I'm sure if Miss Marsden's with them they won't do anything reckless. I think the best thing is to go on with the game and not alarm the others. Miss Marsden's sure to let us know something as soon as she can.'

'It's very troublesome of them, though. I shall have something to say to Dan when he gets back,' Dr Brydon promised, putting her finger at once on the author of the prank.

'And to Charlie Carter. Always up to mischief he is,' Sister Jones announced wrathfully.

'Let's wait and hear what they have to say before we pronounce judgment,' Mr. Cameron advised. 'And now, better get on with the game. The children will be wondering what's wrong. Come along, Katy Dollan: it's your turn to bowl. And, Clara Cox, you take Dr Brydon's bat. She was well and truly caught out by that splendid catch of Mrs Hallam's.'

The game proceeded calmly and with much good humoured fun, but it was not till it was nearing its end that the players sighted the cart that was conveying Miss Marsden and the missing members of the party to the shore.

As soon as they had said good-bye to Jim Hughes, and Miss Marsden had tried in vain to press a reward upon him for all his kindness and help, the adventurers set off to join the rest of the party. Dan and company were a little doubtful of the reception they would receive.

'There they are, all waiting for us on the beach, Mother and Mr Cameron and all,' Dan said, feeling a little guilty.

'And Sister Jones! I say, she does look as if she's got the light of battle in her eye,' Charlie commented, trying to walk normally to disguise the fact that he had lost one shoe.

'I – I think Mother looks a bit grim, too,' Dan faltered.

Miss Marsden could not restrain a little smile, though she soon assumed a becomingly serious expression again.

'After all, you'd no business to wade across to the island like that, you know, Dan, without telling people where you were going. It was rather thoughtless, and it might have led to very serious consequences.'

It was rare for Miss Marsden to speak so severely, and Dan looked rather crestfallen.

'I'm sorry, Marsdie. We didn't mean to be a trouble, really,' he apologized rather miserably.

'We were all in it, truly, Miss Marsden,' Charlie Carter told her, willing to take his share of the blame.

'Here comes Roger. He's the first,' Dan said unhappily, for, indeed, Roger's stern expression was forbidding as he came striding across the beach towards them.

'What on earth possessed you to go roaming across to the island, Dan, you little owl?' he demanded.

'It was a very foolish thing to do, son,' Dr Brydon said gravely. 'We've been most anxious. Anything might have happened to you.'

'You might have been cut off by the tide,' Mr Cameron pointed out.

'We were, Mr Cameron. That's what stopped us from getting back,' Sam Mitton told him with his usual blunt honesty.

'Dear me! Dear me!' Mr Cameron remarked, too taken aback to say anything else.

'Well, Charlie Carter? What have you and Juan to say for yourselves?' Sister Jones asked them fiercely. Then, before they had time to reply, her gaze fastened itself on Charlie's shoeless foot.

'Indeed, to goodness, Charlie Carter, what have you done with your shoe, you bad boy?'

'I got my foot fast in a cleft in the rock, and I couldn't get it away with my shoe on,' Charlie explained to her, looking very shame-faced as he told his story.

When Sister Jones heard what had happened she looked even more cross than she had done before, but whether this was on account of the missing shoe, or whether it was because of the fright she had on Charlie's account as he told the story, it was difficult to say; for beneath her stern discipline, Sister Jones had a real fondness for the Cockney lad and his cheerful grin.

'Well, you've missed the cricket match, and I think you and Juan should miss the bathing party, too, and you deserve it,' she declared with half simulated annoyance.

'I hope we haven't missed tea, too?' Charlie, the irrepressible, asked with real anxiety.

'Tea! If I had my way, Charlie Carter, you'd get bread and water for your tea, for running off like that,' Sister Jones cried.

Miss Marsden felt this to be just a little bit severe, seeing all that the boys had had to endure on Little Hilbre. 'They've really had rather a tough time, Sister Jones,' she pleaded for them quietly.

'We have indeed. We've even been locked up,' Dan informed the company. He was not without a certain thrill of pride in his adventure, now that it was safely over.

'Locked up? Good gracious, Dan, what do you mean?' his mother cried, in perturbed astonishment.

'It's rather a long story, but the boys weren't entirely to blame,' Miss Marsden put in. 'They got lost on that middle island in a mist. You haven't had the sea mist here. It stopped short between the islands and the shore, luckily. But it was owing to the sea mist that the boys met with rather an uncanny adventure on the island.'

Mr Cameron interrupted her gently. 'I think, perhaps, while the rest finish off their game of cricket, and those who want to bathe go off to the bathing-station with Miss Jones, Miss Marsden and these four young scamps had better tell us their story quietly. I vote we adjourn to Westgarth so that we can hear all about it before tea, and then —' his eyes twinkled a little '— and then we'll sit in judgment on these rascals and see if they deserve any tea. Eh, Sister Jones?'

Dr Brydon was quick to see the sense of this suggestion. 'Yes, you'd none of you be the worse for a quiet rest and an early cup of tea with it. What do you say, Marsdie?'

'A cup of tea? Lead me to it,' Marsdie said with enthusiasm.

*   *   *

The telling of the story took quite a long time, and Dan, as principal narrator, had to repeat parts of the adventure several times and to answer a lot of questions for the benefit of his listeners. It wasn't till the real tea for the whole party was ready that he came to the end of the tale.

'So that's how it all happened, right up to where Marsdie and Simon and Mr Thomas came and rescued us, and you know the rest. But weren't we jolly glad to see them!' Dan concluded.

'Good gracious, Dan, you might have been on the island all night – at least, if Marsdie hadn't taken that trip up Grange Hill with the binoculars,' Ruth pointed out.

Roger added with some self-satisfaction, 'Yes, and it's another mercy that I reminded Marsdie to take the binoculars with her.'

Marsdie chuckled. 'But you know, Roger, if it wasn't for my scatter-brain, we'd have brought the camera instead. I got quite a lot of teasing, didn't I – and no doubt I deserved it – but perhaps I might venture to say that the binoculars have been more useful than the camera!' she twitted him slyly.

Roger clapped his hands to his head. 'Mercy me! I've

clean forgotten to take any photographs. We must have some snaps before the light goes. There's just time before tea.'

As Roger was preparing to bundle everyone out of doors, Mr Cameron said, 'I think there's one person to whom you all owe a vote of thanks for your rescue, and that's Dog Jonathan. If he hadn't been able to lead Miss Marsden and Simon to your prison, you might have been there still.'

'So we might,' the four boys agreed. Jonathan looked a little surprised at all the patting and petting he received, and simply couldn't understand why Roger had to have him in the forefront of every photograph he took. At last all the groups were taken, not forgetting a triumphant one of Mrs Hallam holding the cricket ball aloft, in the attitude of Ajax defying the lightning. Then, to everyone's joy, the gong sounded for tea at Westgarth.

Mrs Hallam was soon bustling round in her usual sphere, settling everyone into a place.

'My! What hungry looking faces everyone's got!' she exclaimed. 'Come on, Dan and Sam, Charlie and Juan. You'll be proper clemmed after all your adventures on that island. And you missed your bun and lemonade, too, poor lambs!' Mrs Hallam commiserated with them.

'Poor lambs, indeed!' Sister Jones snorted.

Charlie Carter gave a wink at Mrs Hallam. He had, by now, entirely recovered his spirits, and was beginning to think there was something heroic in their exploit.

'Sister Jones thinks we ought to have bread and water, Mrs Hallam,' he told her with a pretence of being aggrieved.

'Nay, nay, love, she doesn't really,' Mrs Hallam replied

soothingly. 'As my mother used to say – and she was a wise woman – "If there hadn't been a few wild adventurous lads, America might never have been discovered". Come, lads and lasses, pull your chairs up and help me to pass round the cups.'

*   *   *

Tea was almost over and Sister Jones, having now entirely forgiven Charlie Carter, was doing her best to press him to have the last iced bun, with every hope of success, when the door bell rang. Mrs Hallam went to answer it and returned beaming, a rather shy Mr Thomas in her wake.

'Here's Mr Thomas, the coast-guard,' she announced, and quite a burst of clapping greeted Mr Thomas, for the whole of the party had learned by now of the part he had played in rescuing the boys. Mr Thomas looked rather bashful and gave a backward glance to the door, as if meditating an escape from this embarrassing applause, when Mr Cameron came forward, shook him warmly by the hand and led him into the room.

'I didn't want to disturb your party, sir,' Mr Thomas apologized, 'but I've come to redeem my promise to Dan. I've some news for the boys and Miss Marsden.'

Dan started up. 'Oh, Mr Thomas, did you catch that man, Dawson?'

'Yes, Dan,' Mr Thomas nodded. 'Three policemen, with my help as well, soon had Little Hilbre searched and our quarry run to ground among the rocks. It was Dawson, right enough, as I thought. You'll be interested to know, Miss Marsden, that we've just brought him ashore and the police have taken him in charge.'

'Eh, mister, will he have to go to prison?' Charlie asked.

'I expect so,' Mr Thomas told him.

'What for? For locking us up?' Sam wanted to know.

Mr Thomas shook his head. 'No, Sam, not for that, though he deserved it on that account. He's more likely to be had up for being concerned in a burglary not quite two years ago, when some valuable jewellery was stolen.'

'Jewellery! A burglary!' everyone exclaimed in astonishment.

Mr Thomas went on to explain. 'On the way across in the boat, Dawson confessed to the police that he was the man who stole the O'Connell jewels in Liverpool.'

'The O'Connell jewels!' Mr Cameron gasped in surprise, for it had been a particularly daring burglary, taking place when the O'Connel mansion was full of people, and had excited much newspaper comment at the time.

'Yes, sir. After the theft, he buried them on Little Hilbre.'

'Little Hilbre!' the boys cried.

'His buried treasure!' Dan exclaimed.

'Exactly, Dan,' Mr Thomas nodded.

'But you said the burglary took place two years ago. Why did he leave the jewels on the island for two years?' Dan inquired. 'It seems a bit daft to me.'

'Ah, that was because shortly afterwards the police caught him red-handed at another job of house-breaking, and he did eighteen months in prison. He came out about a month ago.'

'But he's had plenty of time to dig the jewels

up in a month! Why didn't he?' Charlie asked, puzzled.

'*Because he'd forgotten exactly where he'd buried them,*' Mr Thomas told them with marked emphasis. 'You see, Dawson was a cat burglar, and when he did that last burglary, he fell twenty feet from a roof and injured his head. That bang affected his memory and turned him slightly crazy, too. He knew the jewels were on Little Hilbre, but for the life of him he couldn't remember exactly where, except that it was somewhere in the old diggings.'

Dan whistled in amazement.

Mr Thomas continued. 'He could only dig at nights, and when no one else was on the island, so, as it was August when lots of people picnic on the islands, he couldn't get on very fast. When the mist came up this afternoon, he never expected any visitors to the island, and your arrival put him out a lot.'

'Yes, he thought we were spies,' Juan said.

'That's right, my lad. He was just a bit crazy, and he had the notion that the police were trailing him all the time. It came from a guilty conscience, I suppose. Well, it's an ill wind that blows nobody any good. Your little misadventure this afternoon helped to bring a criminal to justice and to recover stolen goods. The police haven't searched for the jewels yet, but there's no doubt they're there and that a systematic search will bring them to light.'

'Then I was right after all,' Charlie cried triumphantly: 'there *was* buried treasure on Little Hilbre, even if it wasn't the kind we expected. Wasn't it lucky we went exploring?' he cried, decidedly pleased.

'My word, Charlie Carter!' Sister Jones warned him, shaking her fist, and Charlie had the grace to say no more.

'Thank you very much for coming to tell us, Mr Thomas,' Miss Marsden said gratefully. 'Like Charlie, I'm feeling a bit cock-a-hoopy at the result of the adventure. It's a lucky thing my binoculars saw as much as they did from Grange Hill.'

'Aye, it's a feather in everyone's cap, ma'am,' Mr Thomas agreed. 'We'll maybe all get a bit of credit for what's happened, and I'm grateful to you and the boys for my share in it. Well, I must be getting back to my duties on the island, so I'll be saying good-bye to you all, and I hope you have a pleasant journey back.'

Amid much hand-shaking and promises to come again and visit his island, the St Jonathan's party took leave of Mr Thomas.

'We shall certainly have something to talk about on our way home,' Mr Cameron remarked, looking at his watch. 'We've just time for one more game before we pack into the coaches. Shall it be "Follow my Leader" out of the garden and over the sands? As you're the hero of today's adventure, Charlie, suppose you borrow a pair of sand-shoes from someone and lead the way with your con-certina?'

'I'll lend you a pair, Charlie Carter,' Sister Jones rather surprisingly offered. 'But no paddling out to Hilbre in them, look you,' she laughed.

'You're a sport, Sister Jones,' Charlie Carter said fervently.

So, to the tune of *Follow the Band*, the whole party joined in procession after Charlie Carter, who, with Sister

Jones's hands on his shoulders, jumped like a faun over the sands, waving his concertina up and down, and followed by the dancing tail of St Jonathan's children, laughing and singing behind him.

THE SPLENDID JOURNEY

Honoré Morrow

'. . . . . a tall boy, thin as a shadow, his ragged red shirt tied up with bits of rope to keep it from dropping altogether from his body, his feet wrapped with strips of oxhide, a boy whose long hair fell over his shoulders and whose blue eyes were startlingly large and clear in his tanned face.'

This is John Sager, described during his long journey along the Oregon trail, with his younger brothers and sisters. Set in the America of the 1840s, this story is founded on fact.

These are other Knight Books

THE FLYING FISH ADVENTURE
THE SECRET OF THE HIDDEN
POOL
THE FOURTH KEY
YOUNG JOHNNIE BIMBO

Malcolm Saville

Four 'Michael and Mary' adventure
stories set in different parts of the country,
by one of the most popular writers of
stories for children.

Ask your local bookseller, or at your
public library, for details of other Knight
Books, or write to the Editor-in-Chief,
Knight Books, Arlen House, Salisbury
Road, Leicester LE1 7QS